Warning Signs

Volume 1

by Kate Mageau

Writing, design, and artwork by Kate Mageau
Published by Kate Mageau

© 2022 Kate Mageau

I dedicate this book to New Beginnings, and all its participants I have stood alongside in our journeys to not only survive, but thrive.

TABLE OF CONTENTS

Warning Signs

Prologue

I wrote this book to help people learn the warning signs of intimate partner violence (IPV) and domestic violence (DV). IPV is a subset of DV, as IPV is abuse between intimate partners or spouses and DV is abuse between any family members. Abuse is one person's intent to exert power and control over another person. It can take the form of physical, sexual, emotional, financial, or psychological acts or threats of violence. (For more, see the United Nation's page on domestic abuse.)

This is my personal story of enduring abuse and how I eventually left. After each chapter in the story, there is a section called "warning signs" that discusses the warning signs of abuse that I did not see at the time. When I experienced this abuse, I did not know what DV, IPV, or abuse really was, and thus I did not know what I was experiencing or that I needed to leave the relationship. I wrote the warning signs sections after each chapter to help people see the signs in the context of abuse as it occurs. At the end of each volume, there is a list of warning signs for quick retrieval.

My hope is that this book can teach people the warning signs so that people can: 1) Not enter abusive relationships; 2) Leave if they are in them; 3) Help people notice if someone is in an abusive relationship, and then teach them the warning signs so they leave; 4)

Help people whose loved ones have experienced abuse understand what happened and why it was hard for them to see the signs and leave; and 5) Create a global discussion so that we can change these patterns, so as a society we can work toward ending abuse.

It is critical that we, as a society, do something to stop abuse. In the United States, one in four women, and one in nine men, will experience DV in their lifetimes (cited from the National Coalition Against Domestic Violence). Even if my book helps just one person reach safety sooner than they otherwise might have, I will consider it a success.

I spent seven years writing these books. In those seven years, I attended a domestic violence advocacy support group where I learned about abuse, later I went back as a volunteer to run that support group for two years, saw a mental health counselor who helped me emotionally process what happened, and went to graduate school to become a mental health counselor. I am currently in my final semester of graduate school and an intern at a counseling agency that specializes in trauma, focusing on domestic violence. I have experienced and studied this topic for more than a decade.

There is one more point I would like to address before beginning the story. I refer to people who lived through abuse as "survivors" because we are alive. We literally lived to survive the abuse. This is a much more empowering term than "victims." The victim mentality keeps people living in the mindset of being a victim of something that happened to them, while the survivor mentality helps people realize the strength they have that kept them alive. Some people actually are victims, though, and those are the ones that did not make it out alive.

This is a very important distinction to make because using this term gives those fortunate to survive, survivors, a feeling of power. Early domestic violence resources called people victims, or worse yet, wife-batterer victims. Intimate partner violence does not just happen to wives; it happens to people of all genders and relationship statuses. I am a survivor. Anyone that has experienced abuse who is still alive is a survivor. Throughout this book, I will use the term "survivor" to refer to anyone that has experienced DV or IPV.

As a community of people reading this book and people that care about survivors, I hope that we can help people make smart decisions. Share your thoughts and stories using #WarningSigns so we can grow together.

Volume 1 Prologue

I originally wrote this story as one book, but there is so much emotional content and information about abuse to share, that it felt easier to digest broken up into three volumes. Volume 1 shows the story about how we met, fell in love, and began our relationship together. In some ways, it reads as a romantic-comedy love story, as that is how it felt to me at the time. But looking deeper into it, one can see that there were warning signs that he could be abusive even at the beginning. This is one of the main purposes of this story, and this volume in particular. Looking closely into what people say and how they act can illuminate signs of their character. By learning to identify these warning signs early on, we can hopefully avoid entering these relationships in the first place.

Volume 2 shows the story of our marriage, how our relationship changed, and why I stayed with him. Volume 3 shows how I began to understand what was happening, started questioning my trust in him, and eventually left him. It can feel frustrating to the reader to see how long that takes, but it is really what happened and it is common. It takes survivors an average of seven times to actually leave their abusers.

I hope you learn a lot from this story. There is a lot to take in, so take your time with it and find ways that help you process what you are learning. Journal your thoughts or experiences, talk about them with trusted support people, see a counselor or body healer, draw, paint, create music, dance, or join the online community and share your thoughts and healing processes on social media with #WarningSigns.

Chapter 1: Beginning

When I turned 25, I found myself in a quarter-century life crisis. I heard all my life that to be successful I needed to go to college, start a career, meet a man, wait two years to marry him, buy a house, and then bear children. I felt as though that was the only way to achieve happiness. Yet I had only accomplished step one.

I know, I know. Privileged, white, middle class, able-bodied, heterosexual, cis-woman problems. But that was all I knew at the time. Society told me what I needed to focus on, and I listened.

I earned a bachelor's degree in psychology, and after a short stint in the corporate workforce I went to beauty school. I had always dreamt of being a hair stylist and salon owner, so I set out to make that happen. Unfortunately, I finished beauty school in 2008 and began leasing a chair to run my own business in the beginning of the 2009 recession. All my clients, or their partners, were getting laid off. I had a steady stream of clients, but with their sudden drop in income they all needed to push back their appointments or stop getting their hair done all together, which in turn dropped my income too. My dream of being a hair stylist was becoming futile.

I was also struggling in the romance department. I went on a lot of dates, but every guy I met said he wasn't looking to settle down. I couldn't understand it. I was dating guys around my age… Didn't they want to follow their life plans of success and get married? Yet, none were ready. They all said they wanted to travel and date several women, not marry one and buy a house with her.

In the summer of 2009, I began dating a friend whom I had a crush on since high school, Oscar. It was glorious – he was as sweet a boyfriend as he was a friend. Dating him was everything I had hoped it would be. But within a few weeks of dating, he told me he didn't want to get married, buy a house, or have kids. Sigh. He was like every other man I dated.

He did, however, talk fondly of adoption. He was the first person our age I knew to ever broach the subject. He said there were enough people in this world, and we didn't need to selfishly add more just to propagate our own genes, yet he might want to raise a child one day. Might. He wasn't even sure of that idea. I, on the other hand, found the concept of adoption noble and selfless, and the possibility excited me. I loved it. I didn't love his hesitation though.

I eventually changed my list of goals to accommodate adoption: Step One, college degree; Step Two, get married; Step Three, buy a house; Step Four, have one biological child; Step Five, adopt a child. However, he was against Steps Two through Four due to society's implications of necessity. I was beginning to fall in love with him, yet I was confused. How would I continue my path of success with someone that didn't want to follow that path with me?

I put that aside for the next few months, while he helped me with the career part of my life plan. I worked through high school, college, and beauty school, and then when I finished all my schooling, I had to keep a second job just to pay my bills. I was exhausted, and my salon was getting quieter by the day, so I worked at a chain salon in the mall, hoping to make more money. But after a few months, I was still working two jobs and I was exhausted. I didn't want to give up on my dream, but I didn't have any more energy for it.

Oscar, and my dad, separately suggested I get a job in the corporate world, with benefits and a salary so I would only work 40 hours a week. After years of 70-hour weeks, this concept was breathtaking.

I smiled broadly, "Yeah, I think I would like that." And then I paused. "But how? All my experience is in restaurants, retail, and salons, and my degree is in psychology. I already tried looking for psychology jobs and they all require master's degrees."

Oscar smiled back. "Just start at the bottom, like anywhere else. You were a host before you were a server, right? Apply for entry-level jobs at companies that sound interesting to you, and then work your way up until you find a career you like."

I thought he was brilliant. I didn't know what jobs or companies I would like, but I did know I wanted to make sure I stayed in the Seattle area if I eventually got a promotion at headquarters. I grew up in the Seattle suburbs and went to college in a rural area of the state, and I hated both the suburbs and the farm town. I loved college, but the small-town doldrums and political climate bored me. I loved Seattle's thriving night life, progressive politics, and proximity to my family. I knew I could get eventually get promotions, and that it was possible I'd move for work one day, so I wanted to ensure when that happened, I could return home.

I found an online list of corporations headquartered in the Northwest, and one by one I went to their websites and applied for all their entry-level jobs. There weren't as many options as I had seen in the past, since it was 2009 and the economy was still sinking. However, I wasn't picky, so I applied to nearly everything I saw – which amounted to around 200 jobs. I was eventually offered jobs at two companies, one a cell phone provider that would have hired me as a bill collector, and the other, a travel company that would have hired me as a sales agent. The former was a short commute from home. The latter was in a city almost an hour away, which required me to move and make new friends.

I couldn't see myself being happy as a bill collector, so I accepted the job as a travel sales agent. I found an adorable apartment in a historic building from the 1900s with a view of Mount Rainier, just half a mile from my new office. I loved walking to work, and it kept me in great shape. I was feeling and looking great, and excited for what opportunities this new job would bring me.

Step 1: College degree, check. Step 2: Career, check. Step 3: Marriage. Uncheck. I would have easily married Oscar one day, but he didn't agree with marriage and wasn't ready to settle down.

A week after I moved to the new city to start my new life, and just a few months after dating Oscar, I eventually conceded that I needed to break up with him. I told him, "I'm falling in love with you, Oscar, but I can't be with you if we don't want the same things."

The tears in his eyes mirrored mine and he looked at me sweetly. "I'm falling in love with you too, Kate. But I understand. We might as well end things now before it gets more difficult."

Hearing his feelings for me summoned my personality trait that had been as equally helpful as harmful. My relentless perseverance. Once I settle on something or someone I want, I do everything I can to make it happen.

I squeaked out a small voice and tried to find the courage to be persistent yet strong enough to know when to walk away. "Well, my aunt and uncle were together 10 years before they got married. Maybe, one day, do you think will you change your mind? I can wait!"

He sighed and let out a small chuckle. "I don't want to make you wait for me. Go with your instincts."

We hugged, cried, and said goodbye. Ironically, he is now a married homeowner with a child, and my aunt and uncle are divorced. Funny how life changes.

Chapter 1 Warning Signs

Welcome to your first warning signs section. This is only the first chapter, and at this point we have not met the other main character yet, so there are not any true warning signs.

I want to acknowledge here how I was so firmly set on achieving my life goals. I think this is good, but only when you choose those goals for yourself. My goals for "success" were good goals to have, but the problem is that I thought I needed them for survival, as opposed to things that would have been nice to have. I think my dedication to achieving this success was part of what blind sided me.

However, in no way am I victim-blaming myself. It is never appropriate to blame someone for staying in an abusive relationship, under any circumstances. I am only pointing out here that if I was not so focused on the goal of marriage, then I might have felt less emotionally dependent on him and perhaps left him sooner. It is important to recognize that everyone has their own reasons for staying in abusive relationships, though much of the reasons are that the abuser emotionally manipulates the person to stay with them. These warning signs sections will also show reasons why I stayed and how difficult it was to leave.

Warning Signs

Chapter 2: Meeting

I started my new career at TravelCo in July 2009, in a month-long training class with 15 peers. We were all new to selling travel and we quickly bonded, and several of us started hanging out every night after work. Being in a new city, and not close enough to see my old friends on a regular basis, I found great comfort in this.

One day, the trainer brought in two students from the previous class to talk to us. Jason and Clint answered questions about what it was like to work there, and they made jokes. They were adorable and hilarious. Jason had sandy blonde hair, light brown eyes, and a charming smile. Clint had brown hair, blue eyes, and a friendly smile. They were both about average height, but Jason was slightly smaller and thinner than Clint, who had more muscles.

My friend Jessica looked at Clint and said to me, "Ooh, that guy on the left is hot!"

"Yeah!" I looked at Jason. "But I think the other guy is cuter!" We jokingly set dibs on both of them.

When we started taking travel sales calls, I found excuses to ask Clint and Jason questions, finding the fine line between damsel in distress and competent employee.

"How do I 'Save as?'" I asked him as I face palmed myself on the inside. I may have played up the distress part a bit too far.

Nevertheless, Jason, the resident Excel expert, eagerly came over to my desk to help me every time. He patiently answered my "questions," and then made small talk and flirted. Every day I asked a few more questions, and he lingered a bit longer to answer them.

One evening after work, Jessica organized for us, all of our training class friends, and Jason and Clint, to go out for happy hour. I was so excited to hang out with the cute boys at work! Having spent my first career after college amongst predominately women and gay men, I'd never met any eligible men at work before. I felt like my life was becoming a movie about an empowered, career-driven woman finding love!

The more I got to know Jason, the more I liked him. He told me all about his mom, dad, and two sisters; he described them with love and seemed excited about their lives. I loved that he was close with his sisters, as I believed it helped him understand women better than most men. I told him about my family, and my sister, Kristina, and sparks between us flew. He was about a year and a half younger than me, so it seemed we were at the same places in life.

One night I invited our group of friends to my apartment. Jason noticed *The Godfather* (Puzo, 1969) on my bookshelf and became elated. "You like *The Godfather*?! Those are my favorite movies of all time!"

"Oh," I said as I pursed my lips and lowered my shoulders. "Well, I didn't really like the first movie I saw so I didn't bother watching the rest of them. But I loved the book! It's so descriptive and exciting! Did you read the book?"

He hadn't, but he went on and on to tell me about how great he thought the movies were. I listened and was intrigued by his enthusiasm.

Our friends noticed we were deep in conversation and flirting and decided they would go out for a smoke to leave the two of us alone. I had recently quit smoking, so I had no interest in joining them, but Jason still smoked. He took our friends' hints and decided to stay inside to talk to me. I thought it was nice that he chose to spend time with me instead of smoking. We sat down on the couch next to each other and slid closer and closer to one another every few minutes.

I was – and *am* - bold and confident, and I was on a plan to achieve "success," so I decided to lean in and kiss him.

I was met with a pleasant surprise as he passionately kissed me back. We kept kissing, and a few minutes later we heard our friends knock at the door. We looked at each other and laughed. I raised an eyebrow at him.

He raised one back and asked, "Do you want to let them in?"

I kissed him again and then let out a hearty laugh. "Um, no?"

We yelled through the door, "Go home! We're going to hang out!"

I could hear our friends eye rolls through the door, as they laughed. "Okay, but we need our purses!"

We unlocked our lips just long enough to give our friends their belongings and say goodbye, then we went back to passionate kissing.

After that night, we spent nearly every night at either his apartment or mine, and a few days with friends and family. I enjoyed every minute with him. His sense of humor, intelligence, and playful nature made him infectious. I couldn't get enough. Yet, I still needed to make sure I wouldn't be wasting my time with him.

One morning while he drove us to work, in a confident yet slow and cautious voice I asked him, "Do you want to get married one day? Not necessarily to me, or now, but is marriage something you want?"

He excitedly jumped up in the driver's seat. "Yes!"

My heart leapt for joy. "Okay, great! Me too!" I then cautiously asked, "What about buying a house... and having kids?"

"Yes!" He said again, as he jumped even higher. He turned to grin at me before he shifted his eyes back to the road. "It makes financial sense to buy a house; my dad is an accountant so he's always telling me about this. And I love kids! My mom is a preschool teacher and sometimes I help her in the classroom, and it's really fun!"

"Okay, one more question. Do you like to travel, do outdoor activities like camp and ski, and have random spontaneous adventures?"

"Of course! I went to Greece last summer and it was the best time of my life! I really want to go back!" He told me all about his adventures in Greece.

I was smitten. I breathed in deeply and exhaled with a calm grin. I finally met someone I really liked, and we both wanted the same things for our futures. We talked more about kids and discovered we both wanted a biological child, and he was open to the idea of adopting a second child.

He seemed perfect. Smart, cute, fun to be around, loved family, and most importantly – wanted a family. Check, check, and all the checks. I was happy. Beyond that, we shared the same work schedule, so we could flirt all day long and hang out all night. We were inseparable.

One beautiful summer, weekday morning, Jason's roommate told us he and his girlfriend were renting a boat on Puget Sound for the day. Our part of the country didn't have many sunny, warm days, and I always strived to make the best of them. Plus, I loved boats and being on the water! I raised my eyebrows and voice and said, "Let's call in sick and go with them!"

He was very diligent when it came to work and told me he didn't like taking risks when it came to work. "Oh, hmm, do you think we should?"

I laughed in delight. "Hell yes! Let's go! It's the perfect temperature outside, and we have friends that want to enjoy it on a boat! Let's join them! You said you like random adventures, right? This is one!"

"Ah, hmm, I don't know... I've never called out of work before."

I laughed again, with slight cynicism. "Really? I do it about once every couple months. We have to take the time to enjoy life. We get sick days, right? What if we looked at them as mental health days, and took the time to enjoy life before we got too sick to feel miserable about life?"

I knew my point of view wasn't typical of modern Americans. But it worked for me. I didn't think we needed to sell ourselves to the corporate world, to debtors, or to anyone else. I wanted to whole heartedly live and enjoy life. Perhaps I was naïve in that respect. I often consciously made decisions to enjoy the moment, even when I knew would later have consequences. At this moment, my only goal was to enjoy the journey while I worked toward my goals of success.

Somehow, Jason finally understood my desire and need for spontaneity, if only in this very moment. "Okay, I guess if it's just for one day..." He slumped his shoulders in resign. "Yeah, I guess I'll go."

I was already standing, and literally jumped for joy. "Yay! Okay, let's go!"

His roommate and girlfriend joined me in celebration, and we prepared to leave.

Jason said that before we could go on the boat, he wanted to stop by his parents' house to borrow a cooler. I had never met his mom, Cassie. I wasn't mentally prepared for this part of the adventure. Yet, I was also excited. *Who was she? What was she like?*

He called her on the way to let her know we were coming. I could hear her scold him through the phone. "You have to give me more notice than this! I'm not ready!"

He laughed back, "Mom, it's fine! Really! You always look great. We'll be there in five minutes, and just for a moment to say hi."

I heard her sigh, "Harumph," into the other end of the phone.

Cassie opened the door. She was beautiful. I couldn't easily see Jason's features in her, but they were both good-looking. She warmly greeted me, "Hi! It's so nice to meet you! I'm so sorry I wasn't prepared…," she said as she shot Jason an evil look. She smiled broadly at me. "But please, come in, come in!"

Jason laughed and kissed her on the cheek, "It's okay, Mom, you always look great. I'll go grab the cooler and we'll let you get back to your day."

"Okay, honey," she said to him. And then to me, "Is there anything else you need? Just a cooler? Do you have sunscreen? Do you know how to swim? Do you need a life jacket?"

I laughed. "We're all set; thank you. And yes, the water is pretty cold out there. I think I'll jump in for a second and then climb right back in the boat."

Cassie laughed hysterically. "Yes, it's cold! Are you kidding me?! You're going to get in the water? I was just asking for your safety! But you actually plan to swim?!"

I shrugged my shoulders. "Yup. But it's August! If I can't get in the water now, when can I? I might as well enjoy it, if even for a second!"

She shook her head in disapproving disgust. "I'm from California. This water isn't the beach, and it isn't warm."

I laughed, trying to ease her awkward tension while trying to figure out from where it came. "Well, sure, of course it's warmer in California. But we live here, and I want to enjoy life where I live! I love the water, even if it's cold!"

She laughed back, more relaxed this time, but shook her head at me as though I was delusional. "Okay, I guess." She rolled her shoulders back and took a breath. "It's just... I'm from California," she repeated.

"Oh, okay. How long ago did you live there?"

"My parents moved us here when I was twelve," she sighed and said with resentment.

I took a half-step backward. She had children in their late 20s, so I knew she had to at least be in her 40s. *She had lived in Washington for nearly 30 years, and she hadn't accepted it yet?*

"Oh, okay, well, um, do you like it now that you're here?" I tried not to laugh at the word "now," but I wasn't sure my face succeeded. I quickly looked around the room to avert my gaze and hide my facial expression.

At that moment, Jason came through the garage door. "Hey guys!" he said cheerily. "I found the cooler!"

We smiled back at him, glinted flickers of winks to one another, and said polite goodbyes. Cassie and Jason seemed to care a lot about each other, but there was something weird to me about her yearn for California. Then again, I recognized we're all hung up on something. I appreciated her care for her son above anything else. Besides, I was excited for a boating adventure!

Jason, his friends, and I had a great time together on the water. We enjoyed the sunshine, cool breeze, and occasional freezing cold plunge into the Puget Sound. Jason stayed in the warmth of the sunshine.

Back at work the next day, though, Jason said he felt guilty for calling in sick. I reminded him that it's okay to occasionally take a break and have fun. He eventually made peace with it and told me he took a personal oath to never miss work again. He took his job very seriously, and I admired his loyalty and work ethic. He always wanted to be responsible. I always wanted to have adventures and continue my journey ahead.

Chapter 2 Warning Signs

In the last two chapters I wrote about previously not having met many people ready to commit to a relationship. I also didn't meet many eligible men in either real life or dating online. I saw the fact that Jason wanted to get married, buy a house, and have a family as reasons to be with him; instead of looking at his actual personality characteristics. This was more of my determination to find love and plan my future than a warning sign.

Jason and I both wanted to spend every day together from the very beginning, which was the beginning of our codependency. Codependency is when two people become dependent on one another for emotional and life satisfaction to the point that they lose the ideas of themselves. Codependency is a warning sign of abuse, because in abuse one person controls the other. In an abusive relationship, this is actually more dependency than codependency, yet at the beginning it looks like codependency.

For more information on this, I recommend reading Codependency No More by Melodie Beattie (1986). Jason and I spent nearly every day together immediately, we had the same friend circle, and we worked together, so we quickly became enmeshed in one another's lives. Codependency is a result of a toxic relationship, but it can be hard to see when both people seem to be feeling the same ways. At this point, the codependency felt like falling in love; it felt happy and exciting. The actual codependency will become clearer in later chapters.

This is a good place to introduce the concept of love bombing. Love bombing is a tactic that abusers use to get a person to fall in love with them. They begin the relationship showering the person with love and affection, which makes them feel special, which increases their endorphins and chances of quickly falling in love. Examples are: Quickly saying, "I love you," buying gifts, constant compliments, lots of calls and texts, telling you both are soulmates or fated to be together, asking for early commitment, not respecting boundaries, needing your energy and attention, being intense, and making you feel the love is not equal (Healthline, 2021). Jason and I equally gave each other a lot of love, affection, and time, and intermingled our lives so in our case it was more codependency than love bombing. I included this for information, not necessarily because it pertains to this story.

When I told Jason about my love for the book, *The Godfather*, he ignored me and talked in depth about the movies instead of the books. People often do this when they get excited about a topic, so I did not think anything of it. However, looking back, this might have been one of the first signs that he was selfish.

When his mother, Cassie, told me about how she still missed California after living in Washington for nearly

30 years, I found it a bit awkward. It is not necessarily a warning sign, but it could be a sign that his mother was unhappy, which could have affected Jason and the way she raised him.

This part of the story is only the first few weeks that we met, so there weren't really clear warning signs besides our enmeshment. To me, at this point, everything felt perfect, and I was falling in love. This is why it is so important to recognize and understand the warning signs of abuse as soon as they appear.

Chapter 3: Falling

Jason and I quickly fell into a comfortable weekly routine. We went from spending most every night together just the two of us, to a few nights at his apartment together, a few nights with friends, and three to four nights with his parents at their house.

At first, I thought it was nice, and sweet that he was so close with his parents. We went there right after we got off work at 9:00 pm. But I was annoyed we never ate dinner first, and we were normally there for a few hours. I was always hungry, and Jason never seemed to care. When I brought this up on the way home one night, he said, "Sometimes I forget to eat; it's not a big deal."

I responded, "It's a big deal to me. We need to eat dinner after work. I can't wait a few hours to eat. Our bodies aren't supposed to do that. We ate lunch almost six hours ago." He was used to drinking a quad-shot mocha for breakfast, smoking cigarettes for lunch, and eating fast food for dinner. Those 2,000 plus calories at dinner must have been enough to keep him full through the next day. I preferred to eat small vegetarian meals throughout the day, so we had a hard time understanding each other's metabolisms.

Eventually, he said he agreed to allow us a few minutes to stop by a grocery store and get something to eat on the way to his parents' house. Once we did that, my mood and interactions with his family improved.

Things were going really well, and I liked getting to know his family. The more I fell in love with Jason, the more I wanted to know the people that raised him.

I loved our casual evenings together, yet in the back of my mind I desired a romantic date. I wanted to dress up and eat a nice meal, and gaze into each other's eyes across the table. We hadn't done that yet.

I said to him at work, "Hey, so I think we've been dating for about a month now... When, do you think, is our one-month anniversary?"

"Oh, hmm... Late July? Early August? I don't know the date."

"That's what I was thinking too, but it would be nice to have a real date on the calendar and a real romantic date. Maybe we can look at receipts from the first night we went to happy hour?"

Proud and determined, he practically shouted, "I don't keep receipts, but we can check bank statements!"

"Great idea, honey! You're a genius!"

I investigated and then exclaimed with glee, "July 28th! Great teamwork! So, okay! August 28th is next weekend! Let's celebrate! Let's go have an actual date and celebrate!"

We went out for dinner and drinks, and a great time laughing and talking. That night, I realized how happy he made me.

We looked into each other's eyes, and I squeaked out a whisper.

"I love you."

He looked at me with surprise and delight, and asked, "You love me?"

I lowered my eyes, nodded, and then looked up with hopeful hesitation.

Then he grinned and replied, "I love you too."

That was it. Nothing could stop us from being together.

I also realized that if we were going to be together, I needed to voice my opinions. I enjoyed spending time with his family but a few nights a week with them and once every other week with mine wasn't fair.

I finally spoke up. "Hey, can we see my family more often? I like visiting with your family, but I miss mine."

"But they're almost an hour away! It's too late to see them after work!" he complained.

"I know, but we could see them on weekends," I persisted.

"Okay, yeah I guess we could do that."

The following weekend, we visited my parents, and we all had a great time. I appreciated the way he listened to me and took actions to make changes. Life with Jason was great.

Once we fixed the eating issue, and spent time with my parents, I still couldn't understand why it bothered me to spend so much time with his parents. We could have spent time together with friends, with my family, adventuring… the possibilities seemed endless yet fruitless. I felt my sense of comfort taking over and my sense of adventure slipping.

A few weeks later, I asked him, "Do you think it's normal to spend so much time with your parents as an adult? I'm close with my parents, but even when we lived in the same city we saw each other weekly, not three to four times per week."

"Yeah, of course it's normal! I love them so why wouldn't I want to spend more time with them? I love you and I see you every day; is that weird?"

"I guess not then," I replied, not totally sold on his answer.

The next week, I realized it wasn't just the frequency that frustrated me. Jason's Dad, Adam, and Cassie held different religious and political opinions than I, and I felt like they thought their viewpoints were the only valid ones. Jason fell somewhere in the middle of us all. I didn't judge them for our differences, though I did have some challenges with not being able to calmly share opposing opinions.

It was the fall of 2009, and Congress was debating the ACA, the Affordable Care Act. Adam and Cassie were furious about it. Jason tried to look at it from both sides and refrained from sharing his opinion. I believed, and still do, that we need universal health care, and the ACA was a step in the right direction.

Adam said, "This is just going to make it harder for businesses to stay afloat, since they have to pay for their employees' healthcare."

I defended the ACA. "What about all of the good it will do, though? I think it's fantastic that everyone will have health insurance. And I'm sure the business owners will find a way to make things work. CEOs make millions of dollars, so they just need to spend some of that money on others instead of themselves."

Adam was outraged I would say such a thing. "Those CEOs worked hard to be where they are. They deserve what they make. And what about the smaller companies, where the CEOs don't make as much money?" He said, practically snarling at me with disgust for not understanding the plight of the business owners.

He went on to explain Cassie's and his views. He said they thought everything should be privatized to create market competition and therefore provide plenty of low-cost choices. They said they agreed everyone should receive healthcare, but the government didn't have the right to affect how the healthcare companies do business nor force businesses to provide it.

I didn't think the ACA was perfect, though I knew it could help a lot of people. My close friend Eric had one of the largest hearts of anyone I knew. He was also born with an enlarged heart and died the year after the ACA went in effect. He changed jobs and wasn't able to get health insurance because he had a pre-existing condition, and therefore wasn't able to get his prescription medicine. His fiancée found him on the floor one day. She later told me Eric had been getting his prescriptions through a friend who was a black-market drug dealer. He couldn't reach his dealer that week. If the ACA had been in effect just a few months prior, Eric might still be alive today.

So, when Jason's parents argued that people should continue to access healthcare through their jobs, I vehemently disagreed and didn't hold back from saying so. This conversation was a year prior to Eric's death, yet I still understood the principle of equal access. It seemed Adam spoke for his entire family, and he simply echoed sentiments from his favorite news channel.

I was furious. "Are you saying that the people who don't work for large enough companies to receive healthcare don't work hard? They don't deserve healthcare. Besides, if your concern is for smaller businesses, the law says those with under 50 employees don't have to pay for health insurance."

I admit I was probably looking at Adam like he was a complete idiot. He would have been an even bigger idiot if he couldn't read that on my face. However, that wasn't my intention.

He turned to look at Cassie and Jason with a big sigh. He then squarely looked me in the eye and said, "Perhaps we shouldn't discuss politics."

Taken aback, but still trying to be polite, I took a deep breath and said, "That's perfectly fine. We can talk about anything else."

We sat in awkward silence for a couple minutes.

My parents taught me to think for myself and question everything. Our political conversations deepened my knowledge of the world, as we asked questions for understanding. As a 4-year-old, my most commonly used word was, "Why?" But in Jason's family, Adam echoed the news he chose to watch and then taught his family to echo *his* words.

Jason attempted to formulate his own opinions and told me them in private. But in front of his parents, he either voiced support — or nothing at all. He gave in to their desires of cohesive family opinions instead of challenging them.

Jason eventually decided he would break the tension by going out for a cigarette. Even though I didn't smoke, I usually joined him outside. I enjoyed the crisp fall evening air and space away from his parents.

He jumped and paced around the front yard. Suddenly he turned to me and echoed Adam, "Maybe we shouldn't discuss politics with my parents anymore."

"Yeah, I guess not," I responded with despondence. I paused to think. Then I rolled my eyes and said, "I didn't realize they were more concerned with CEOs' welfare over others."

"Oh no, that's not true," he insisted. "My Dad is in finance, so he always looks at things from a fiscal perspective. My parents are fiscally conservative and socially liberal. I'm pretty liberal too, but I do tend to lean fiscally conservative."

I made my peace with agreeing to disagree. Otherwise, his parents seemed to be sweet and welcoming.

The next week, Cassie, Adam, Jason, and Jason's sister, Diana, and I talked in the living room. Jason and Adam walked to the hallway, and I followed behind them a minute later. As I left the living room, I heard Cassie say to Diana in a perfectly clear and audible voice, "I miss Stacy. She was so sweet."

Diana emphatically agreed, "Me too!"

Stacy was Jason's ex-fiancée. My heart dropped.

I asked Jason about it later. "Did you hear what your mom said?"

"No, what did she say?" He asked perfectly casually, as though nothing happened.

"She said that she misses your ex, and Diana agreed. Don't you think that's a weird thing for them to say when I am here? Do they not like me?"

"Oh no, they think you're great! You just have different opinions than they do, and they're still getting to know you."

"Okay. Well, I don't plan to keep my mouth shut about my opinions if politics come up again, so hopefully they don't. I'm entitled to my own opinions."

He rolled his eyes and took a step backwards. I narrowed my eyes at him, and he understood my look to show that I was serious. He stepped in to kiss me. I thought, *This is how he shows me he loves me, even if sometimes he disagrees with me.*

After that, I decided it was more important to keep my political opinions to myself unless I was expressly asked, so I could get his parents to like me. I figured that even if they were a little frustrating and uncouth when expressing their political views, I still loved him, and he wasn't his parents.

Chapter 3 Warning Signs

Jason did not seem to care that I needed to eat dinner after work, and it was strange that he did not feel he needed to either. When we left work and I asked him about dinner, he would always ask me to wait until after we saw his parents. But we saw them for a couple hours, so by the time we ate, I was starving. It seemed he did not notice or care about my need to eat dinner, which is a human need. The way he handled this shows me that he was selfish. A kinder person would have made sure both of our human needs were met instead of ignoring them. It should be a baseline expectation that a partner wants to make sure their partner is not hungry.

I told him I loved him on our one-month anniversary. He told me he loved me too, which at the time made me feel ecstatic. However, falling in love that quickly was a warning sign of the codependency we were already forming.

He did not even consider that I would want to spend time with my family too. Once I explained that it was possible to see them on a weekend, he agreed, although it seemed like a reluctant after thought. In this section, I wrote, "I appreciated the way he listened to me and took actions to make changes. Life with Jason was great." I was grateful that he listened to me and made changes, which is nice, but in a healthy relationship with a kind person these wouldn't have been changes we would need to make. We would have both already asked each other about the other's needs and have made decisions together. At this early in the relationship, it is a warning sign if the person is not respecting your needs, and a sign they may be selfish.

The political disagreement with parents could have happened in any relationship. The way that Adam and Jason told me that we shouldn't talk about it anymore, though, made me feel they were telling me to shut up. It might work for some people to just not talk about politics in their families, but this isn't how the situation made me feel. I agreed to it because I wanted to get along with his family. I ignored the way they silenced me because that felt easier. This is a warning sign that I did not listen to my intuition about feeling uneasy being silenced.

Cassie and Diana's clearly audible conversation about Jason's ex-fiancée in my ear shot was rude and disrespectful. Jason and I talked about it, and he made me feel better after that conversation. However, his family should not have had that conversation when I could hear it. It felt they were trying to tell me they liked her better, which made me feel insecure.

A huge warning sign I missed in all of these interactions with his family is that I ignored how his family treated me. They were disrespectful. In a healthy relationship, people's family members treat one another with respect. If I had paid attention to the way his family made me feel, I would have talked to Jason about it more and then decided whether or not I wanted to be part of his family. I never truly considered being accepted by his family and how that might affect our relationship down the road; I only focused on my relationship with Jason. I also never considered that being in a relationship means being accepted and respected by a partner's family. They frustrated me, but I always accepted them as his family and treated them with respect. Jason could not change his family, but he could have stepped in to ask them to be kinder. Or, we could have decided that since his family didn't seem to like me, that we would end the relationship at that point. But I decided to stuff my feelings and move on with my relationship with Jason.

Chapter 4: Joining

Jason and I continued to spend every day at work, and every night after work, together. The nights we weren't with his parents, we played pool, went to Irish bars, played a video game where we played musical instruments, or invited friends over. We always had a great time and never wanted to be apart. Sometimes when our friends were over for several hours, Jason and I told them we were "doing laundry" and snuck off to the laundry room to physically be together. We were very excited about how the first three months of our relationship were going.

We initially took turns spending nights at each other's apartment. But, when I was home alone at my apartment, I often heard gun shots. I didn't feel safe at my place by myself. Jason and I decided it was best if we stayed at his apartment more often.

I was also never really comfortable being by myself. Ever since high school, I spent all my free time with friends or boyfriends. I felt bored, restless, and anxious when I was by myself.

It was comforting to be with Jason every night, and I adored that he wanted to keep me safe. So, we spent every night at his place, and every morning I waited for him to shower and get ready, and then we drove to my apartment, and he waited for me to do the same. It got tiring after a while, and sometimes when we were at his place, I wanted something from my apartment, like a sweatshirt to keep me warm and comfortable.

One morning that September, when we were leaving his place, I asked, "Hey, would it be okay if I kept my sweatshirt here, so I don't have to bring it back and forth?"

He shrugged his shoulders, "Sure, of course. Why not?"

I was surprised at how easy his response was, considering all the previous commitment-phobe men I had met. I smiled and slowly said, watching his expression, "Okay, well what if I also left a toothbrush?"

He chuckled. "Sure, babe, you can leave whatever you want here."

"Thank you!" I said with a kiss.

The next morning, I said, "Hey, so we spend a lot of extra time in the mornings waiting for each other to get ready. And if you don't mind if I have a few things here... What if we lived together?"

He beamed. "Sure! Let's do it!"

I was so shocked that I laughed. "Really? You're okay with that? I mean, you want to live together?"

He laughed back. "Of course! We spend every night together anyway, and we would save time and money, so why not?"

I smiled and then suddenly felt nervous. I had never lived with a boyfriend before. My only other serious boyfriend was in college, and he constantly pissed me off, so I consistently broke up with him every month. Then I always got back together with him when he convinced me to do so. He's a lawyer now. Go figure. So, Jason was the first boyfriend with whom I wanted to live.

I asked, "Wait, but are you sure? Are we ready?"

He kissed me on the cheek. "Oh, you're cute. Yeah, babe. We're ready. Let's do this!"

I kissed him back. "Okay!"

The next day we made arrangements with our landlords. I moved into his apartment the following week. He never really liked his apartment because it wasn't new and modern, but I loved it. It was in a historic building in the center of the city, and it had heart and character. I felt safe and happy there.

I also felt safe and happy at work. I loved selling travel to people, and its only minor downside was that it was so easy I was often bored.

We worked for TravelCo in a satellite office about an hour away from headquarters. In late October of 2009, just four months after I started working there, everyone in the office received an email invitation for a mandatory office-wide meeting. We worked on the phones, so it seemed strange for the entire office to go to a meeting at once. There was a thick layer of fog that day, and the temperament in the office mirrored it.

At 2:30 p.m., around our usual lunch time since we worked late shifts, we all gathered for the meeting.

Someone in a very high position in headquarters greeted us. We never thought we would meet someone so high up the corporate ladder. It felt weird he was there, and even weirder he wasn't smiling and excited to meet us. We all felt the tension in the air.

He began, "We want to thank you for all you've done here. You've had amazing sales and you've all done a great job."

He took a deep breath, paused, and continued. "We called this meeting to let you know we are closing this office and outsourcing it to The Philippines. We have a sales and service office in Las Vegas, and we encourage you to apply for jobs there."

I heard a collective gasp and then whispers from every direction. I was solemn, lost, confused, frustrated… I felt the gamut of emotions. I was still new, and I had spent the previous six months looking for a new career. I spiraled back into a depression of the unknown.

Jason, on the other hand, turned and looked at me with the utmost glee. "Vegas???!!! We can move to Vegas???!!! Let's do it!! You want to go, right?" I had never seen him so excited.

He tried to infect me with his enthusiasm, but all I could feel was dread and panic. I couldn't stomach it.

I went to college in a tiny town on the other side of the state. I only moved back to Seattle a few years prior, and I loved living in the city again. I loved the culture, the liberalism, the arts, the nature, and most importantly, that I was close to my family. I was happy here, and I hadn't planned on ever moving again. The city we lived in wasn't quite as big or great as Seattle, but it was close in feel and proximity.

I cautiously replied, "Um... sure... I don't think I want to go, but let's talk about this later. Let's see all of our options."

He pouted but obliged for the moment. When we left the meeting, he excitedly talked with our friends and colleagues about moving to Vegas and tried to convince everyone to go. I silently observed our friends point out the downsides of moving to and living in Vegas, and Jason illustrated the perks.

"It will be so much fun! There's sunshine! And 24-hour bars! And strip clubs! And pools! And so many shows and clubs!"

Their moods seemed to be close to mine. They each said things like, "Um, sure, but it will be hard and expensive to move. And I like it here. I like having all four seasons and a more wholesome environment."

They went around and around in their disagreements, and I held out hope for Jason to see their points. Jason's mind couldn't be changed. He spent his childhood summers in inland California with his recently deceased grandmother about whom Cassie and he often reminisced. The dry heat and desert made him nostalgically happy. Plus, he loved to party. He loved Las Vegas.

TravelCo gave us a three-month settlement, in which we still received our paychecks and still had benefits such as health insurance. We were not in a big rush to make a decision, but we knew the recession was continuing to worsen and it was a hard time to find a job. In the following weeks I stopped trying to talk him out of moving to Vegas, and instead focused all my energy trying to find a job at home. I was determined to find a better opportunity, to prove to both of us we could be happy in careers at home. I spent five hours a day searching for and applying to jobs. In the four short months since the last time I applied for jobs, the options dropped. None of the corporations were hiring. Nonetheless, I searched, applied, and kept up my spirits.

Jason, on the other hand, was determined to go to Vegas and spent those same five hours playing video games. I didn't care for video games to begin with, but he was so enthused by it that I supported what made him happy. Yet, he spent most of his time playing games with graphics so life-like that the violence was nearly impossible to watch.

I did, however, find it frustrating that he wasn't looking for jobs with me. Occasionally I suggested he do so, and he refused to look for anything at home. He said he loved his job in sales at TravelCo and he wanted to move to Las Vegas, so he only applied for sales jobs at

TravelCo Las Vegas. He said he didn't want to work for another company, so I looked for jobs for him at TravelCo's headquarters in a nearby city.

Every time I read a job description, he asked, "Does it require a college degree?"

They always did, so I tried to encourage him and said, "You know, managers often write a wish list on their job descriptions, and they still hire someone if they only meet some of the requirements."

He shook his head. "No, babe, it's not worth my time," and resumed attention to his video game.

One day, he sat down and looked at jobs with me. We ran into the same issue. It was tough to argue with him; the job market was tight. We were in the height of the recession. He only needed to take two more classes to finish his AA degree, but we both knew that the time it would take to finish those classes wouldn't have made much of a difference in his immediate job prospects. He reassured me he was happy working in sales. I suggested he apply for sales jobs at other companies at home.

He shook his head, and then shouted, "Let's go to Vegas, baby!"

I gave up the argument and decided to leave it up to my hard work, determination, and fate.

After I didn't hear from any job for three weeks, I realized how bad the economic situation was. I decided to partially give in to Jason's desires. I said to him, and the universe, if I get a promotion at the TravelCo Vegas office, then I would take the job and move. I bit the bullet and applied.

I heard back a few days later, and interviewed the next day, on a Friday in November. They offered me a job on the spot. I would be a Level 3 Senior Agent and represent the corporate office as the third level of customer support. I would research errors and resolve customer problems. The job sounded interesting, and management assured me this role would be the quickest path to further growth opportunities. It all sounded great, but I was still not thrilled about moving to Vegas, especially with someone I had only been dating a couple of months. Yet, since I hadn't heard back from anyone else, that seemed like my only option. They were excited to hire me and wanted my answer by the end of the week.

Jason picked me up from the interview. "Hi, honey! How was the interview? Did you get it?" He asked excitedly, while kissing me on the cheek.

"Hi," I said in the cheeriest voice I could muster. "Um, yeah. They want me to tell them if I'll take it by Friday…" I trailed off, not sure how I felt or what else to say. I could have elaborated about the perks and pay of the job, which were admittedly good, but I didn't want to give him more ammunition for Vegas.

"Congratulations!!!!! I'm so happy for you!!! Great job!!! Yay, we're going to Vegas!"

I meekly half-smiled back and thanked him. I added, "I haven't totally decided yet. I want to wait a little bit longer in case I hear from one of the jobs I applied to here. And, well, if I don't get one, I could always get two retail jobs or move in with my parents again... Although I really want to be an adult and figure this out on my own."

Rent prices in Seattle hadn't yet soared to their second tech-era boom, but they were still too high for most entry-level jobs. I worked two jobs to afford my last apartment, so I knew I was capable, but I really didn't want to do that again. Mostly, though, I wanted a plan that included staying with Jason.

"Oh, okay honey. But Vegas!!! We can go to Vegas! Vegas, baby, Vegas!" Earlier in the week he insisted we watch the movie *Swingers* (Independent Pictures, 1996) to get in the "Vegas spirit." It was a fun movie, and I laughed at his joke while admiring his enthusiasm. Ever since, he couldn't resist saying, "Vegas, baby, Vegas," at every chance he got.

"You're adorable," I said with a kiss. "I just need time to think about this, though, okay?"

"Okay, baby. Let's go celebrate! We can at least celebrate the fact that they offered you a promotion, right?" It wasn't really a question.

"Haha," I said flatly. Then I tried to lift my mood, so I changed my tone and said, "Okay, honey. Yes, you're right. Thank you. Besides, I'm hungry and I could use a beer."

We stopped at home, and I walked in the door and looked around at our studio apartment. I gazed at our picture window with 1920s molding looking out to the downtown neighborhood and park across the street. I studied our kitchen with cool vintage, black and white tiles. I looked at our bathroom and the claw-foot bathtub. I stared at our living room, where we spent countless nights hanging out with our close friends.

Suddenly the apartment seemed to spin. I felt nauseous. I loved our apartment and the the Northwest's quintessential Evergreen trees. I wasn't ready to leave, but I didn't know what else I could do to find a job or convince Jason to stay. Our other friends from work told us they decided to use unemployment benefits until they got a job. Jason's parents balked at that and said they were lazy. They made it clear that should not be an option for us and shamed our friends. His parents also tried to convince me to get on board with us living in Vegas because it made Jason so happy. My parents, though, were supportive of any decision I made.

I looked at Jason, and he seemed concerned, yet still excited. I admired his positivity, but at that moment it wasn't appeasing me.

I went in the bathroom and threw up. I felt stuck. After a few minutes of heaving, I took some deep breaths, cleaned myself up, and reentered the rest of the apartment. Jason asked if I was okay. Without pausing for a response, he told me a friend was meeting us to celebrate so we should go and not keep him waiting. My moment of reflection and panic expired. I put on my best "happy" face.

We had dinner, and the whole time Jason and Clint talked about how great Vegas was. Clint also worked at TravelCo but had decided to stay in the Northwest. He was more than happy to help Jason convince me to go with him, though. It was November, so it was about 45 degrees Fahrenheit, cold, and rainy. This was the typical northwest weather I knew I could expect until March.

Jason showed me the Vegas weather report. It was 70 degrees and sunny. As freezing cold as I had been feeling lately, that sounded nice. They reminded me that most places have pools there, so we could swim and enjoy the weather year-round. They reminded me of Cirque du Soleil shows and all the entertainment in Vegas. They reminded me how inexpensive it was to live there, so we could easily have enough money to get a two-bedroom apartment to host family and friends, and still have enough to frequently fly home to see them.

Jason had been to Vegas once or twice before with family, and he loved it all: The sun, desert, gambling, strip clubs, and the fact that he could drink and smoke indoors.

I loved the blue water and green trees of the Northwest and didn't understand his affinity for the desert. He reminded me of his nostalgia for the desert and memories with his grandmother. I also didn't mind gambling or strip clubs, but I wasn't excited about them and certainly wouldn't move somewhere because of them. I quit smoking about a year prior, so didn't care that people were allowed to smoke inside. I joked with him that it would cause him to smoke even more frequently. He laughed and said that wouldn't happen, with a slight glint in eyes alluding the opposite.

He was really excited about the move. I could get on board with sunshine, swimming and Cirque shows, as long as I could still frequently see my friends and family. I finally agreed to a compromise: I would apply for a few more jobs and wait to see what happened. If I hadn't heard back from anyone by the end of the week, then I agreed to move.

On Wednesday around 1 p.m., Jason heard back from the sales manager in Vegas. They offered him a job in sales. Soon enough it was Friday. One week since they offered me the job. The day had come. I still hadn't heard back from anyone in Seattle or any neighboring cities. I waited until 4 p.m., just in case someone called for an interview. Tick. Tock. Tick. Tock.

At 4, I took a deep breath. And another. Finally, I called and accepted the Level 3 job. Jason almost bounced off the walls. My hands shook. He barely stopped jumping long enough to notice my fright. He sat by my side and hugged and held me. He reminded me how much we love each other and how much fun we would have. His love made me happy, and after a few minutes in his embrace I felt supported and relaxed.

He excitedly told me, "We're in this together, babe! I know it's going to be hard, but we will get through this together!" I believed him.

Chapter 4 Warning Signs

Jason and I moved in together after only three months of knowing one another. That is incredibly fast, even for most healthy relationships. I knew it was fast, but I was also scared of the gun violence where I lived, so at the time I felt I was making the best decision for my safety. He and I were spending every night together anyway, so it also seemed appropriate for us and our relationship. This is another warning sign of codependency. I could have found a different apartment by myself, moved in with my family, found roommates... I could have made a variety of different decisions that would have been better, but I was set on my life plan and that included being in a relationship that I believed held promise for the future.

A possible warning sign was that he only played violent video games. He played games with realistic-looking people where he scored points for killing them. Just playing those games is not enough of a warning sign, but the fact that he only played those types of games very well could be one.

Another aspect to consider here is that he agreed to live with me after only dating for two months because I suggested it. Abusers tend to agree with whatever their partner wants in the beginning, so later they can get what they want, and possibly use this is a negotiating term. But, at the time, I didn't see that anything was wrong.

Getting laid off and being forced to either find a job at a different company in the 2009 recession or to move to Las Vegas only made this quick move-in decision more complicated. Once Jason heard about the opportunity to move to Las Vegas, he made up his mind. He did not even try to find jobs at home, even though that was what I told him I wanted. He never truly had an open conversation with me about it. He never considered what I wanted, which is another warning sign showing how he was selfish and only cared about himself.

I eventually succumbed to his needs and applied for a job in Las Vegas, even though I didn't really want to. I was already feeling codependent and intricately involved in a life with him, so I applied for the job because it was the only solution that would keep us together. Once I got the job, he acted as though the decision was made. Except, I hadn't made the decision. I literally felt so conflicted that my stomach twisted and turned the same way my mind was. He ignored both my uneasiness and my desires, which was another warning sign of him being selfish. But I loved him and ignored my instincts, even when my body was telling me something was wrong. This is also a warning sign. It seemed easier to be swept up in his infectious joy than to push against it and fight for my own needs. I eventually gave in because I didn't want to be apart from him. I had grown dependent on him for meeting my emotional needs and "success" needs of a relationship.

Once I decided I would make the move with him, I ended up doing all the research and setting everything up for our move. He didn't help with any of our moving plans, besides getting a friend to drive us, and he didn't help pack anything. I saw it as him being lazy, and perhaps unaware about what needed to be done, but I knew what needed to be done so I did it. This was also a warning sign about him being selfish. He didn't help, and he didn't act like it was a partnership.

In a healthy relationship, both partners would discuss their wants, needs, goals, and emotions. Then they would make a decision together. I attempted to have these conversations with Jason, but he dismissed them, and I found it was easier to go along with what he wanted instead of fighting. I didn't realize it at the time, but this is when I began slowly losing myself to him; a definite warning sign.

Chapter 5: Journeying

Once we decided to move, I began to prepare. I read countless articles about neighborhoods in Vegas and looked into countless apartments. TravelCo paid for us to go on a house hunting trip, so I mapped out apartments for us to see.

We looked at a few apartments in different areas. The first few we saw were inexpensive and also in walking distance from a few grocery stores and restaurants. They weren't super nice, but I was fine with that. Jason was not.

On our second day of apartment hunting, we saw a great apartment right across the street from our office. It was in the nicest, safest neighborhood, and it was a cute, modern apartment. The one downside was the office was the only amenity in walking distance. I asked the leasing agent if there were any restaurants or anything else nearby.

She answered, "Well there's a Burger King about a quarter mile away."

Good food has always been important to me, and I never liked fast food nor considered them to be "restaurants." Jason's family thought I was a food snob, but I knew I cared about food quality and my health.

I responded with hesitation and as much tact as I could muster, "Um, yes, I saw that. Are there any actual restaurants?"

She looked surprised at my response, and furthered, "Yes, Burger King is a restaurant."

Jason said, "Babe, that counts!"

I smirked and tried to hide my disdain. I shyly said, "Well they serve food there…Okay, I guess that's a no then."

Our prospective apartment had a fireplace, a patio, granite counters, stainless steel appliances, a built-in dishwasher, and an in-unit washer and dryer. Our previous unit didn't have either of the two latter features, to which Jason had lamented.

"Babe! A dishwasher *and* a washer and dryer?!"

I gently tapped his arm and whispered, "But where will we 'do laundry'?"

He laughed. "Maybe at the clubhouse with the gym and sauna?"

I laughed back. "Sold."

The apartment complex had a beautiful pool with a rock feature waterfall surrounded by jasmine blossoms and lush green grass, set amongst a backdrop of dramatic, red-orange desert mountains. All of this was $400 more than the other units we saw, but only $200 a month more than we paid for our barebones-amenities studio apartment back home. I didn't want to spend more, but he convinced me. Then we were both excited, so we negotiated down the lease $100 less and signed it.

When we returned home, I scoured the internet for the best deal on a moving truck, utilities, and everything else we needed to know about the city. Jason found a friend to help us drive the truck, which was helpful since I couldn't drive, and he didn't feel comfortable driving a moving truck 1,100 miles in the winter.

The last week at home was the last week of December. TravelCo brought me into train at the satellite office full time that week. We were ready for our move, but also needed to plan our Christmas together, which included visiting my mom and Stepdad, my dad and Stepmom, Jason's parents, and Jason's grandparents. All our family members wanted to see us, and we also had to pack and work. We ended up figuring it out, but none of our family members were completely pleased with how little time we had for them. Jason expressed relief and a part of me agreed. It was stressful trying to please everyone. He reminded me that our families could visit us when they wanted, and we could do the same. He repeatedly mentioned that he looked forward to having time for just the two of us without the stress of other people's opinions and scheduling time for everyone, and admittedly the idea seemed kind of nice.

I felt as though I was operating on an incredibly high frequency, with no way of grounding myself. I felt stressed and anxious about the move and all the things needed to be done. When I told Jason this, he sat me down on the couch with him, held me, and helped me calm down and relax. He always told me I needed to relax more. So did my dad, and basically all my male

friends and past romantic counterparts. With my mom
and close girlfriends, though, our conversations always
centered on our levels of productivity and what else we
could be doing to make our lives better. Most of the
females in my life took care of the household planning
and details, and I was no different. It always felt difficult
to relax if I knew there was something that needed to be
done.

In those three days, we had a lot to do. Jason went
out to smoke cigarettes every hour or so to relax, and I
frequently joined him. I soon found myself smoking, too.
I had quit smoking a few years prior, after a previous
boyfriend asked me to stop for him. The temptation and
the ease to smoke with Jason felt nice, and I enjoyed
having the opportunity to talk with him when he wasn't
playing video games.

Sometimes I wished he was as productive as I was,
though. I asked for his help with the move, and he
responded with, "Sure, how about in an hour? Let's relax
together for a little while first," and kissed my cheek. We
cuddled and watched TV together and he was right, I felt
relaxed. But an hour easily turned into two, and a day
turned into a week.

Eventually, I got his assistance for about a half an
hour at a time before he got bored and wanted to go back
to his violent video games. I packed a majority of the
apartment, and he succeeded in packing only his
belongings. I felt better about myself when I was

productive, and confident in my abilities to take care of everything. Yet, I also felt annoyed at how little he helped.

I felt anxious about moving to Vegas and wasn't particularly thrilled about it, but I was excited for the sunshine, and more importantly, to see what Jason would be like without so much direct influence from his parents. I noticed that when it was just the two of us together, he was more relaxed, happier, and calmer.

I had observed in those last few weeks that the more frequently we saw his parents, the more he agreed with them, and the more conservative and strongly opinionated he became, as well as more critical of me and my political opinions. I began to look forward to Vegas more and more.

We celebrated our first Christmas together as I was scurrying around the house packing. He sat me down on the couch and brought me his card and gifts. He bought me a photography book of prominent Seattle locales so I would have a visual reminder of home, a wine bottle opener because I loved wine, and a tiny yet elegant Tiffany's necklace. His mom treasured Tiffany's. She loved it so much she painted one of the rooms in her house "Tiffany blue" and filled it with all her Tiffany boxes from previous holiday gifts her husband bought her. I saw the fact that Jason bought me something from Tiffany's as a demonstration of him loving me as much as his father loves his mother.

His Christmas card to me read:

Καλά Χριστούγεννα για την Αγάπη μου

عيد ميلاد سعيد إلى حبي

It said, "Merry Christmas to my love," in both Greek and Arabic. He learned a little of both languages when he traveled to Greece and relished in the fact that he could read languages in alphabets other than Roman. He wasn't fluent in either language, but he was proud of knowing the alphabet and a few words and basic phrases. I loved how thoughtful his gifts were, and I found it sexy that he knew multiple languages.

Christmas with all our family members was tiring, but a lovely opportunity to see everybody a few days before we moved 1,100 miles away.

The day before moving my parents and sister helped us pack the moving truck and say goodbye. It was a cold, bright, and sunny day in late December. The weather matched my trepidation with optimism. My parents were tremendously helpful and brightened my spirits. We had a lovely dinner afterward. They asked us, as did everyone, "How long will you be in Vegas?"

Jason and I hadn't really discussed this, as we had no idea how long we would be there. He shrugged his shoulders and looked at me with hopeful eyes we would be there forever. I looked back at my family's hopeful eyes that said they hoped we would come back soon.

I answered, "Well, we signed a contract with work that we will be there for at least a year or else we have to pay them back for moving expenses. So, we'll stay a year and discuss it then."

My parents sighed and lowered their shoulders. They briefly glanced at each other, picked up their voices, and said, "Okay, that makes sense." We said our goodbyes and hugged.

The next morning, Jason's close friend, Manny, met us at Jason's parents house to drive the moving truck to Vegas. The night before we had parked the moving truck at Jason's parents' house in the suburbs, so it would be safer than the city and so we could have one last opportunity to say goodbye to them. Cassie was crying uncontrollably. Adam was in a strangely jovial mood. I figured he was happy because Jason was happy. We all hugged goodbye and left. When I hugged Cassie she whispered through tears, "You take care of my boy."

"Oh, I will," I responded with a smile. She waved to us as we left. As we turned the corner, I looked through the side mirror and watched her run into the house sobbing.

Jason sighed deeply. With a nearly undetectable tinge of heartache and despair while trying to sound proud, he said, "I hope my mom is going to be okay without me. I've always been the one to hold the family together."

I rubbed his shoulders and calmly said, "She's an adult, honey. She'll be okay. She still has your dad and two sisters with her in Washington."

"Yeah… You're right," he said as though he didn't quite believe me.

I wondered if that was what made Adam so happy. I thought perhaps he finally felt the freedom to be the "Man of the House" upon whom Cassie could rely. Adam already did everything for Cassie, though. They each had their own cars, and when Cassie's was running low on gas, Adam drove it to the gas station and pumped it for her. He also bought all her clothes, because he enjoyed picking them out and she said she appreciated having one less thing on her plate. She rarely cooked since when she did, Adam, Jason, and his two sisters, often made fun of her for "ruining" the food. Instead, Adam generally picked up food for the family on his way home from work. Adam paid all the bills, did all the household repairs, and even wrote Cassie's work newsletter for her. Once, Cassie used an ATM and the machine ate her debit card. After that, Adam and the kids took turns retrieving cash for Cassie. It looked as though she emotionally held the family together while Adam did everything else. Jason told me he turned to her for emotional support, so much so that both parents told him when they had marital problems. I suspected Adam looked forward to his wife leaning on him instead of her son.

Manny was Jason's best friend. He rode motorcycles for fun, and for a living he worked on cars and drove trucks. Manny was very sweet, despite how often he told people how tough he was. Jason looked up to Manny for his heteronormative skills, and Manny looked up to Jason's intelligence with computers and languages. The moving road trip plan was for Manny to drive the first half of the 1,100 miles and then have Jason take over the rest. We also towed Jason's car behind the moving truck, so it wasn't an easy driving experience. Jason's first car was nearly thirteen years old and had over 160,000 miles on it. He loved it. When people asked him when he would buy a new one, he said, "I'm going to rock this car until the wheels fall off!" It was though he saw his car as an extension of his ego; if his car could survive anything so, could he. He was determined to drive his car as long as it would allow him.

As we approached the halfway point in northern California, Jason asked Manny if he wanted to switch. "Manny, you're doing awesome! Do you want to switch! You're such a great driver, man!" He yawned and continued, "So, how are you feeling?" It seemed he was appealing to Manny's machismo in order to encourage him to continue driving. "Do you feel okay, like you can keep going, or do you need me to drive now?"

"Oh, no I got it," Manny said in a proud voice with a broad smile. Jason was successful.

After we drove 10 hours, I asked Manny, with the voice of my mom's worries about our safety in my mind, "Do you want to stop and rest? I can get us a hotel room with the moving money I got from work." Since I earned a promotion to a higher position in Vegas, I received a lot more moving money than Jason did. I paid for the truck, the gas, food on the drive down, and all the move-in fees for our apartment.

Jason said smugly, "No we're fine; we don't need you to spend your money."

I hesitantly glanced at Jason, and then sort of halfway gave him a side eye. I wanted to acknowledge Jason, but I didn't like how he was manipulating Manny and disregarding my offer to help. There was no reason we couldn't stay in a hotel for a night. We left on December 29th, so if we got there in two days, we would have arrived in the middle of the day on New Year's Eve. We all wanted to celebrate New Year's Eve on the Las Vegas Strip. We started work on January 4th, so we had plenty of time to get to Vegas to party on New Year's, and plenty of time to unpack before we started work. I quickly looked at Manny and asked, "Are you sure you're okay to keep driving?"

Manny puffed up his chest and said, "Oh no, I'm good. I just need to stop and get some energy drinks."

"Okay," I responded calmly. "Well, let us know if you change your mind."

Manny drove all the way to Vegas in one night. It took 24 hours, including truck stops for gas and snacks, smoke breaks, and meals at fast food places. Manny and Jason referred to them as restaurants and savored those flavors, and I was disgusted. I was vegetarian at the time. I have never been a fan of eating processed foods made of chemicals, especially in places where business owners don't typically pay employees livable wages. Since Manny was driving, he chose our meals. Jason was happy with his decisions, and I was outvoted. I focused my energy on feeling appreciative for Manny's eagerness to drive.

We arrived safely in Vegas. We were early, so our apartment wasn't ready yet. We stayed in a hotel a few miles from our apartment. When we received the keys to our apartment, we unloaded the truck and carried everything inside.

I unpacked the apartment, and the boys returned the moving truck. When they came back, and saw all the work I was doing, Jason whined, "We don't need to do this right now... Let's just relax!" He smiled widely and opened his arms for a hug. "You know you just want to relax with me!"

I smiled and hugged him back. I was slightly tempted, but I responded, "I don't actually. We've been sitting in a truck for 24 hours and I want to be productive. And, we only have a few days before work starts and I'd like to have the apartment ready for the work week. Can you guys please help me? Well, Manny doesn't need to, but can you?" I felt the same despondence about unpacking as I felt about packing, yet I was still determined to get Jason's help. I also believed Jason would be different in Vegas without his parents' influence.

"Okay, in a little bit. Let's get coffee first," he offered as a compromise.

We all had a nice time getting coffee and then drove back to the apartment. We drove around a roundabout. A mile down the road, we drove through a second roundabout.

When we went through the second one, we felt and heard something fall behind the car. Jason pulled over. We all got out of the car to see what happened. The hubcap came loose, and the wheel literally fell off the car and spun down the street for a whole block!

Manny and I laughed. Jason's face turned red with anger. Manny patted Jason on the back and said, "Well, you said you would drive this car until the wheels fall off! Are you ready for a new car now, buddy?"

Jason nearly shouted back, "God, no! I didn't think this would *actually* happen! I'll call the auto repair service and find a repair shop." He got out of the car, huffily jumped around, and kicked one of the remaining tires.

We were only half a mile from our apartment, and I didn't want to be around Jason when he was angry. I looked around and realized we were less than a mile from our apartment. I said, "Okay, well I will walk back home and take care of the apartment while you guys take care of the car."

Jason shouted, "Fine! "Thank you for unpacking but *don't* touch my electronics! I'll take care of them!"

I rolled my eyes, nodded, and said, "I know, honey! They're yours and only you know how to put them together." I did my best to give him a half a smile and started down the street.

When I got home, I unpacked the kitchen. In our apartment back home, Jason never wanted to cook, or really even let me cook meals for us; he didn't seem to notice the kitchen was even there besides for a place to hold his beer and energy drinks. Somehow this translated to me seeing the kitchen as my territory, and fixing the car was the men's territory. A few days later Jason was able to laugh about the irony of the situation. He drove his car until the wheels fell off, put them back on, and ignored the signs.

Chapter 5 Warning Signs

I know this is a long chapter. It's the pivotal transition time showing what happened once we decided to move to Las Vegas until we arrived there. There's a lot to unpack. I want to point out that this was still very early on in the relationship – just five months – so even though I was annoyed at some things, I was still very much in love. This is still the beginning phase when abusers don't show their cards, and this really does not happen in an obvious way until the end of the first book. This is typical, and part of why people stay with their abusers for so long. People do not even recognize they are being abused.

What we can look at here, are the unhealthy relationship aspects, and the beginnings of warning signs actually about to appear. Domestic violence (DV), is violence between family members; and intimate partner violence (IPV), is specifically violence between people in a romantic partnership. The Center for Disease Control and Prevention (CDC) includes physical violence, sexual violence, stalking, and psychological aggression in their definition (CDC, 2022). These are not isolated violent instances, though; abuse is a pattern of violence where one person tries to control one another. Yet, one violent incident is a likely sign for more to come.

The Power and Control wheel, created by the Duluth Model (1984), and commonly used in DV and

IPV advocacy agencies, shows all the ways that someone can control someone. See the wheel here:

The idea is that abusers use various manipulation tactics to gain power, and when they gain even a little bit of power, they use that to control their partner, the survivor. This is often followed by the survivor calling out the abuser on their actions, which results in the abuser apologizing and temporarily changing their behavior. This interaction makes the couple feel closer, which most often makes the abuser's power stronger.

Then the abuser generally does something else abusive, the partner tries to talk to them about it, the abuser apologizes, and then repeats their action. This repeats and repeats and each time the cycle gets tighter and tighter, like a spiral turning into a cyclone. This is the general pattern of the cycle of violence. What we can do to defend ourselves is learn this cycle and learn the methods of control. When we learn these, we can identify them and leave the relationships before the cyclone spins so tight that its too hard to leave.

Here are the warning signs from this chapter:

Even though Jason was the one who wanted to move to Las Vegas, I did all the work to prepare for the move: I mapped out apartments to see, I set up and paid for all of the utilities and moving truck, and I did 90% of the packing and unpacking. He was selfish in that he didn't help me do any of the work, even though I was the only one working at a job, for most of that time period. Part of this might also be contributed to his strong sense of patriarchy. It seemed he expected me to do the work. The patriarchy is an unofficial system of society that gives men the power to have control over women. Jason appeared to believe in this, as opposed to an egalitarian society in which both partners share power, or matriarchal in which the woman has the power.

When I offered to pay for a hotel for us on the road trip, Jason said, "No, we're fine; we don't need you to spend your money." This shows me that he was feeling insecure about me paying for everything, which is also a beginning sign of his strong belief in the patriarchy. We can also see this when he made me feel that unpacking the kitchen was my territory and the men fixing the car was their territory, as those are traditional male and female roles.

Jason often mentioned how nice it would be to be by ourselves, without friends or family around. One tactic abusers use is to isolate their partner so that they can have further control over them. When friends and family are not around the couple, they cannot witness the abuse and they are not physically there for the person being abused to turn to go to them for support. That person can generally still call friends and family, but then they are only hearing what the person chooses to tell them instead of seeing the whole picture. Jason never liked it when I called my friends and family when he was home, and consistently tried to get me off the phone with them. I had to strategically call them when he was not around, which gave me fewer opportunities to be in contact and tell them about what was happening.

It took me awhile to understand Jason's family dynamic, and to be honest, I still don't fully understand it. But I know something about it seemed unhealthy. For instance, when Cassie told me, "You take care of my boy," I thought it felt weird. He was a 24-year-old adult, and I believed he could take care of himself. I also thought it was weird that Adam was in such a happy mood the morning we left. I think in a healthy family, parents would feel sad that their child was moving over a thousand miles away.

It is also not healthy that Jason's parents turned to him when they were having problems in their marriage. In a healthy family, parents do not tell their children about their problems or put them in the middle of their issues. When parents do this, they risk the child forming negative opinions of their parents, as well as risk the child feeling responsible for fixing their parents' problems. This can lead to the child feeling insecure about being responsible for the reason their parents have problems, which can also lead to feelings of guilt and shame.

When I was stressed and anxious about the move, I wrote that I was, "operating on an incredibly high frequency, with no way of grounding myself." I wish that I talked to someone about how anxious I felt, so that I could have tried to figure out what was causing the anxiety and then found a way to feel grounded. I think part of the anxiety might have been that I was ignoring my instincts about moving with him. But I chose to stay busy and keep focused on all the tasks that needed to be done. These are not expressly warning signs, but they are things that made me uncomfortable. Any time someone does not feel comfortable about the way they are being treated; they should pay attention to it.

When Jason told me to just relax with him instead of doing everything I needed to do, it annoyed me because he wasn't helping me do anything. He did not take responsibility for himself and the things that we both should have been doing together. Instead, he minimized the amount of things we had to do and minimized my feelings about being anxious. Minimizing is another abusive tactic, and a warning sign. Abusers minimizes their partner's feelings to make them feel that they are not as important as their own.

I clearly saw Jason manipulate Manny to make him do all the driving. He appealed to his ego and faked a yawn to encourage Manny to continue driving. This was not a warning sign of abuse to me, but it was a warning sign that he was capable of manipulation.

The last warning sign in this chapter was that Jason kicked the car tire when it fell off. Manny and I laughed because of the irony that Jason said he would drive the car until the wheels fell off, but Jason immediately turned to anger. I think some anger is natural in that situation, but him kicking the tire was a warning sign that he used physical aggression when he was angry. Around this time period, when we were still in Washington, Jason was using an old laptop to play video games. One day, his laptop overheated, and Jason stood up and yelled. Then he threw the laptop on the ground and stomped on it. It worried me when I saw that, but I figured it was just violence toward an inanimate object. I never thought he would use violence on a human.

Chapter 6: Exploring

We really enjoyed exploring Las Vegas together. The city was intoxicating — we gambled, danced, and drank the nights away. The electronic slot machines each made their own sounds, announcing themselves at seemingly random intervals, with the top 40 songs from the last three decades playing in the background, just barely loud enough to allow my ears to choose to hear, "Eye of the Tiger," instead of, "Play Texas Tea! Test your luck and drill for oil to see how much you can win!" Ironically this was one of my favorite games – I think it seemed the most sinful for someone who cares so much for the environment.

The neon lights of the Vegas Strip were brighter than the sky was dark. In the Northwest, we were accustomed to foreboding clouds hanging over our heads and distilling the night's darkness. In the Vegas suburbs, away from the lights, it was so dark I needed to use my phone to see my feet. On The Strip, though, the lights screamed at us with beautiful sex appeal. They shouted, "Come play! Come into the light!" The glorious neon was like the devil in a bad horror film, enticing us to follow the Sin City lights to sin and descend the staircase into hell. We blindly complied, only subconsciously aware that it was the darkness that would later become our shadows.

After long nights gambling and drinking, Jason typically suggested we go to strip clubs. It was his favorite way to sober up before driving home. We lived in the suburbs, half an hour from The Strip. Transit in Vegas left something to be desired, taxis cost $70 each way, and Uber and Lyft didn't exist yet, so strip clubs felt like an acceptable option rather than driving drunk. Sometimes hotel rooms on The Strip were extremely affordable so we stayed the night. But to both of us, not drinking just wasn't an option in Vegas. The city was appealing and exciting, but too much to handle sober.

The strip clubs were never my first choice, but he loved them, and I didn't mind so I went along for the ride. To my surprise, they were a lot of fun. The first few times I enjoyed simply observing the women dancing. They seemed to enjoy themselves and displayed more confidence than I could imagine. Sometimes I felt jealous of their their beautiful, athletic bodies. I also noticed the male patrons: A majority wore ill-fitting business suits, chain-smoked cigars and cigarettes, and smugly ogled the women while they leaned back in their leather armchairs that peeled apart at the seams. Yet, they all seemed to respectfully enjoy themselves and their views. Once I realized both the performers and attendees were content and respectful of one another, I relaxed and enjoyed the scene. I admired the dancers' abilities to display athleticism and grace, while simultaneously commanding electric control of the room. I spent some nights talking to the dancers, and some nights as a patron getting lap dances. It was a safe place to explore my sexuality, and truly indulge in the "sins" of Vegas.

Partying was how we forgot about work for a few hours. Every night seemed like it was the *only* time we would ever experience fun in our lives. Our new jobs were infinitely more challenging than our previous positions, and therefore caused more stress. We challenged ourselves at work and then again at night, to have the most fun possible. Work hard, play hard, and figure out life lessons through trial and error.

We also had a lot of fun making and meeting friends. Jason made a friend, John, who grew up in Vegas and had a close group of friends. John introduced us to Mario and Lisa, Chris and Missy, and Robert and Tiffany. We all got along really well and hung out several times a week. We also spent time with other friends who moved to Vegas with us, including Mary, Adria, Joe, and David.

Jason loved TravelCo, and was excited to continue work in sales, but the leadership team took several months to set up the Vegas sales department. In the meantime, he worked in customer service, contacting banks to reverse customers' superfluous bank authorizations. He anticipated upselling expensive vacations, and instead acted as a sounding board for irritated customers. We were both frustrated with TravelCo, but we signed agreements we would work there at least a year or else we had to return the money they gave us for moving expenses. We could have left early and paid a pro-rate of our contract, but we also felt loyal to a company that paid us to move and have new experiences.

The Level 3 job I was so excited about turned out to be more difficult than I ever thought. I was told I would have a powerful position that allowed me to help people and use problem solving skills to find creative solutions. The reality was 80% getting yelled at by angry customers, 15% learning DOS-like line-by-line software programs on the job without formal training, and 5% problem solving and appeasing the customer. Level 3 meant I was the third person the customer spoke with to solve their problem, so by the time I talked to the customer, they were audibly upset to the point I needed to move my headset a few inches away from my ear.

My first week I had a customer with a cancelled flight due to weather. She booked her ticket on two different airlines, so I called both airlines to help find her another flight home. The airline operating the flight offered to rebook her on their next available flight – five days later. The airline owning the ticket suggested she pay for a new ticket — for $5,000 — because weather is an "Act of God" and therefore neither airline is responsible for rebooking. I was so frustrated at both of these so-called options. I didn't think either was fair for the traveler. I took pride in myself and my job, and I wanted to give her a better choice. I remained calm on the phone, but I was beyond stressed on the inside. I squeezed the stress ball on my desk with all my might, released it and squeezed my shoulders to give myself motivation. I asked my supervisor for help, and she suggested a conference call with both airlines.

While I was on hold, my shift ended and so did Jason's. Jason came over to my desk to see if I was ready to walk home across the street together. I explained the situation and asked if he had any ideas. He said nonchalantly, "That sucks. Well, just let the customer know." He cocked his head and angled his body to begin walking away from me. He shrugged his shoulders and said, "That's all you can do."

I looked back at him with tears in my eyes, faced my body square to his, and opened my shoulders to emotionally and physically to ask for help. In a high-pitched voice, trying not to whine, I said, "I think you're right. I've been trying to help for four hours, but it's not fair. She has a job and a cat to get back to; she can't just stay on vacation five more days." I put my head in my hands and leaned towards my knees, folding in on myself.

"You've been helping her for four hours?!" He said in disbelief, as he took a step away. "Yeah, just call her back and let her know."

I raised my eyebrows at him and turned back to the computer, pointing to show I was still on hold with the airlines. He knew I did my best to help her, so he didn't understand why I was still visibly upset. He waited 15 minutes for me and then left. I didn't mind walking home by myself, but I wished he stayed for emotional support.

The conference call diminished all hope for a sooner or less expensive flight. I let the customer know and we both held back tears. She thanked me for trying so hard, but I still felt dejected.

Thankfully this customer didn't yell at me, but I was upset with myself. I was still upset when I arrived home and Jason still couldn't understand why. I had worked through all my options but felt there must have been another idea that could have helped. I've never liked accepting subpar solutions, especially when it affects the customer so greatly. Accepting self-defeat and upsetting the customer were even more difficult to deal with when my boyfriend couldn't understand my pain.

Although, he was great at helping me relax and take my mind off work. His favorite distraction method, if we weren't exploring The Strip or hanging out with friends, was to watch movies with associated drinking games based on character verbiage or repeating themes. I preferred to talk out my issues until I felt better, or his understanding made me feel better, but I accepted distraction as a second option. After repeatedly watching the same type of movies with subtle themes such as "damsel in distress" or "stereotypical African-American character," I eventually suggested we watch independent movies and make up our own drinking games based on phrases the characters said. I tried to explain to him the underlying sexism and racism in the Hollywood movies he liked, but he never understood and always told me to "lighten up." He frequently told me I didn't have a sense of humor because I didn't find his sexist and racist jokes funny. I eventually convinced him to let us take turns choosing movies, so I chose documentaries and movies featuring strong female leads. We made up drinking games to those as well, and I enjoyed erasing the workday with creativity, humor, and booze.

Throughout the next few weeks at work, I got more comfortable with the software programs, and finally felt I *sort of* knew what I was doing. The emotional aspect didn't get any easier, though. One day, a customer called because her coupon expired the following day. She said she couldn't use it because she was calling from the hospital where her mother was admitted. I was shocked she bothered to call us in that situation, and I wanted to help her, so I offered to extend her coupon for one month, with the original terms and conditions to uphold the company's policies.

She was outraged. "You're only giving me one month?! I'm calling you with my mother on her deathbed and you're only giving me one month?!"

I apologized for her circumstances and offered two months instead. She questioned me, and I reiterated myself, several times over. I stood strong.

I could have given her a coupon which lasted two years and waived the original terms and conditions, but I was recently reprimanded for giving too many of those away.

The customer hurled back at me, "What is your name?!"

"Kate," I replied firmly and clearly.

"Well, KATE!" she yelled into the phone, loudly enough for me to hear her voice echo off the hospital walls. "I hope you meet a KATE on the day your mother dies!"

I was shocked. She didn't even know me. I was trying to help her and maintain my job. She was the one spending her time calling a travel company from the hospital about a damn $200 coupon while her mother was dying!

I took a deep breath and replied. "Well, I hope I do. I'm a very nice person."

She laughed maniacally and asked to talk to my supervisor. He suggested I extend the coupon for six months. Neither of us wanted to deal with someone so angry, so we looked for an easy way out. The extension was a consolation prize for everyone involved.

Half sarcastic and half appreciative, she said it was a nice offer, but didn't accept it. She guffawed and retorted back, "I SAID I wanted to talk to your supervisor. Not for YOU to talk to your supervisor and come back with this bullshit. Let me talk to him."

I was emotionally exhausted and generally still in shock of how badly the conversation was going. I grabbed my stress ball and lowered my head. I found some inner strength, took a deep breath, and asked if she would hold for him. When their conversation ended, he told me he gave her the 2-year coupon. I felt equally disrespected by the customer and betrayed by my supervisor. I wished he would have had my back and reiterated company policy, but he was more interested in saving himself stress than upholding the rules – an option I did not have.

I had only been in this position two months, and I still had 10 more months in the contract to work at the company. With that kind of daily emotional stress, I knew I needed to find a job that made me happier, even if it meant paying the early exit contract fees. During the next few weeks, I looked for jobs every night. Jason couldn't understand my level of stress and unhappiness. He was annoyed I spent so much time job searching instead of relaxing with him. His lack of support frustrated me, and I knew I needed to be happier. I continued job searching, despite his frustration. I also hoped once I found happiness, then I could inspire him to do the same. He was also miserable at work, but his supervisors consistently told him they would open the sales department the following month, so he did his best to retain his optimism. It took six months.

I figured we have 24 hours in a day, and we ideally spend eight hours sleeping. A workday is eight hours plus a 30-minute lunch break and two 15-minute breaks, so nine total. How do we spend the rest of it? An hour getting ready for work and more to commute. About another hour is spent eating dinner, whether that's cooking or going out. So, add eight hours sleeping, nine hours working, one hour getting ready, and one hour eating dinner; we're only left with five hours in our day, or less if there is a long commute. I surmised, then, as humans that need to work to live, we better as hell enjoy how we spend a majority of our time.

I had a few interviews, but all ended being for similar jobs disguised as something more intriguing. TravelCo was my first experience working in an office, and I had only been with them eight months. All my previous experience was customer service, restaurants, and the beauty industry. And 2010 had finally begun. The economy was getting better, but more and more companies were offshoring their customer service positions. I accepted that I would be in this current position longer than I wanted, but I continued searching. Once Jason eventually accepted that I would be spending more evenings job hunting, he was more supportive. It was a good thing because he was my largest source of happiness at that time.

Chapter 6 Warning Signs

Through the emotionally difficult work experiences, Jason did not show empathy for the customer I was trying to help, or for the stress I was enduring at my job. When I told him about the situation with the customer stuck with the cancelled flight and no reasonable alternatives, he said, "That sucks. Well just let the customer know." He did not seem to understand the stress the customer was in. Thankfully, since then, the airlines changed their policies, so they put people on new flights without charge when they cancel them, but that was not the case at the time.

Jason also couldn't understand why I was still upset when I came home that night. A healthy person would be able to understand that, and if they couldn't, they would listen to their partner until they understood. Healthy people have empathy, and healthy relationships have partners who empathize with one another. The fact that Jason could not understand my emotions or be there for me shows me that he did not have empathy, which was also a warning sign.

Jason frequently told me that I didn't have a sense of humor because I did not think his sexist and racist remarks were funny. On the Power and Control wheel, this is listed under "Emotional Abuse." The relevant parts here say, "Putting her down; making her feel bad about herself." This is the first example that I remember that he did that to me, although it's highly likely there were other times.

Jason was annoyed that I spent time searching for jobs instead of spending time watching TV with him, even though I was there sitting with him. He did not support me in working to find a way to lessen my stress and tried to make me feel guilty for not spending quality time with him. "Making her feel guilty," is also listed on the Power and Control wheel under "Emotional Abuse." A supportive, healthy partner understands their partner's needs and gives them the emotional space and support to do what they need to do. They also often offer help. Jason did none of this. He seemed to only care about his need for me to be relaxing with him.

Emotional abuse is not just a warning sign of abuse, but it is actual abuse. This is often how abusers begin their abuse. Emotional abuse brings down the partner's sense of confidence, which leads to their insecurity. When a person feels insecure and dependent upon their partner, they often become reliant on their partner for emotional security and search for it in the good times when they are getting along. This often leads to the abused partner becoming more attached to their abuser, and consequently not even think about leaving them. This is where the codependency shown in the beginning started turning into dependency.

I ended the chapter with, "He was my largest source of happiness at that time." In all honesty, I really felt as though he was. My job was stressful, but after work I got to come home to him to relax with him on most evenings. I was not only becoming dependent on him, but I was also becoming more and more reliant and dependent on him for my own happiness.

Chapter 7: Befriending

Spring in Vegas was amazing. It was 70 to 80 degrees Fahrenheit March through May, and it felt nearly perfect. The winds were high, as they often reached more than 30 miles an hour, though the breezes made the warm weather sufferable. I loved that I could enjoy my evenings dipping my feet in the pool while flipping through a magazine in March, when it would have been 45 degrees back home. I missed my friends and family back home, but I found joy in that most of the year it was warm enough to host pool parties and barbecues. Jason and I had a lot of fun enjoying sunshine and pleasant outdoor evenings with our new friends.

I was still miserable at my job, though. In May, I heard from a colleague that a business travel division of TravelCo was opening a call center on the first floor of our building and hiring at least 100 people. I had been working in the leisure department, so this was seen as a step up. I applied and interviewed. They were skeptical I didn't have any business travel experience yet impressed with my software knowledge I learned in my current position. I was thrilled that at least some part of the challenges of my current job paid off.

A few weeks later I was hired and in training class. I was a Senior Booking Representative. The "senior" part of the title made me laugh since it was an entry position,

but I liked how fancy my title sounded. The training
focused on a lot of the same software, so it was easy for
me. I helped answer many of my peers' questions while
still in training. At the end of training, we took a test and
I scored highest in the class. Once we began the actual
job, there were some challenges, but overall, it felt like a
breeze. I loved how nice and appreciative the customers
were. Within a few months I was answering colleagues'
questions who had been in the business travel industry
for decades. I felt important. I relished finally being
recognized for my intelligence and abilities.

On top of that, life was going well with Jason. We
had been in Vegas for about six months. We had finally
settled into our lives in Vegas and found a routine. Once
a week we had board game or poker nights with our
friends, one or two nights we explored The Strip, and the
remaining nights we stayed in together. Those nights we
took turns choosing TV shows to watch, and the first
couple hours he played games on his phone while I
learned about things online.

Every few months I found a new topic in which to
immerse myself, such as hypothetical wedding planning
and home buying. I read as much as I could. The last few
hours we cuddled together and paid attention to our TV
shows. I loved the way we laughed at comedies together
while enjoying our own interests online. It seemed he
finally understood my needs to continually learn and
grow. Later in the evenings, when we watched crime

dramas together, he held me, so I felt safe and secure in his arms. I felt truly happy and relaxed. Most importantly, my love for Jason grew stronger and I began to easily envision our future. I felt I had found my happiness.

The next time I had a challenging work problem, I told Jason I needed his emotional support.

"How?" he asked. "By listening to me vent and offering ideas to solve problems in the future. Basically, just talk with me."

"Oh!" he said, with a smile that read pleasant surprise. "I can do that."

He was able to listen to me and talk out my problems with me, and then he learned how to do the same with his problems. Once he got the hang of it, we spent a few hours talking about work every evening, and worked through our work issues together. We both got better at emotionally dealing with work stress and at solving customer problems. Not every day was perfect though. Jason seemed to get more stressed about work than I did, and then we spent a lot of time talking about his issues. It was usually helpful to talk things out, but some days he just wanted to be angry and stay angry even after hours of venting about it. I soon realized it was best just to give him space at that point. Once he was angry it was hard for me to do anything right.

Sometimes just offering him dinner or asking if he wanted to go out and do something angered him. His face would get red, he would narrow his eyes, and yell, "No! That's not what I want! You're so stupid!"

I was initially hurt by this, but quickly learned to deal with it by ignoring his words. I told him not to hurt my feelings anymore, and he apologized, but he repeated his behavior each time he was angry – Which turned out to be every week, and sometimes twice a week. After talking everything out for hours I tried to improve his mood by offering suggestions of fun things to do, such as going to The Strip or hanging out with friends. Sometimes he would accept one, and sometimes he just pouted and called me a bitch. I eventually learned to ignore him until he was in a better mood. But sometimes my suggestions worked and made him happy, so I didn't want to give up. I was never sure what his mood would be when he got home from work, yet I felt that most days were good.

Sometimes we had issues because I cooked dinner. He would yell at me, "I can't even eat this! You don't know how to cook at all! Why do you even bother?"

I *was* just learning how to cook, and I wasn't good yet, but I wanted to keep trying. And I enjoyed my meals. They weren't necessarily pretty, but they tasted good to me. One day, though, I asked my mom, "Should I even bother?"

She gently responded, "Well, do you enjoy cooking?"

Hesitantly I said, "Well, yes… I enjoy being creative and having an outlet, and I like having dinner ready for my boyfriend. But I don't like that he only likes what I cook once a week or so."

"Hmm… Maybe you could talk to him about what he likes to eat, or he could help you cook?"

I laughed, nearly choking. "He won't help me. I have asked him what he likes so many times, and all he says are bacon burgers, chicken strips, and pizzas. That's just not enough variety for me. I've already given up being vegetarian for him, just because it's too annoying to cook two separate meals. I'm not going to give up on vegetables and variety in food altogether."

She laughed with me. "Well, maybe you can discuss some meal plans and compromise with him."

I agreed and thanked her. I suggested the idea to Jason, and he agreed to decide on dinner menus together at the beginning of the week, which greatly improved the situation. I found recipes for simple meals, and sometimes he let me introduce him to new food.

That summer, Jason's best friend, Clint, needed a life change, so he moved to Vegas. He needed a place to stay, so Jason offered our couch in our one-bedroom apartment. I enjoyed Clint's company, so I was happy to help him, yet anxious about the tight living quarters.

It turned out that Clint's arrival was exactly what Jason needed. He instantly brightened Jason's mood. Jason was always excited to get home from work and see

Clint. Clint spent his days cooped up in the apartment looking for jobs, so he was eager to go out at night and explore Vegas with us.

Clint handled Jason's bad moods with impeccable grace and knew how to gently tease him to make him happy again. He also didn't mind when Jason teased him back. They also enjoyed teasing me together, but it seemed harmless the way Clint did it, as opposed to Jason "teasing" me that I don't have a sense of humor or know how to cook. They listened to their favorite songs on repeat, and quickly discovered the most offensive songs were the ones that bothered me the most so those became their "favorite" songs. As long as Jason was happy and not criticizing me, I didn't mind too much. The three of us went out nearly every night. We showed Clint our the spots we liked and discovered new touristy things to do together. It felt as though we were all on permanent vacation.

After a few months, the lack of space for Jason and I became more of an issue for our sex lives than our relationship could handle. We were barely having sex once a week and arguing more and more. Just when Jason and I were almost too frustrated, Clint found a job and his own apartment. The three of us still hung out on a regular basis, and I felt that we all felt emotionally and sexually healthier to be in our respective spaces.

In that fall of 2010, Jason's sister, Diana, and her best friend, Jenny, came to visit. Jason told Clint, "Hey, if you want to hook up with Jenny, I bet she would be down. She's pretty easy. I think she has a boyfriend, but I bet you could still get with her if you want."

Clint laughed and said, "That's okay buddy. That would be weird to hook up with your sister's best friend."

Jason patted him on the back and said, "Just wait till you meet her. Let me know when you change your mind."

Jenny and Clint had an instant attraction to one another and hooked up the last day of Jenny's vacation. When the girls left, Jason said, "See! I knew you could do it, man!"

Clint laughed and said, "Actually I like her a lot. We exchanged numbers and we're texting right now. She says she's going to come back and visit soon."

A few months later, Jenny moved to Vegas and in with Clint. They became close, and the four of us regularly spent weekends together. Jason was happy to have his friend living here, and even happier to see his friend happy. I was also happy having Jenny there. She was super sweet, and it was great having a balanced male-female dynamic.

We had fun adventures together, such as the time we rented a boat on Lake Mead. Somehow, we scraped the bottom of the boat on a barnacle, even though we avoided the barnacle-dotted map they provided. Clint and Jason negotiated with the boat company and the county sheriff to let us go free for *only* a cool grand for repairs. I say this sarcastically, as that was a lot of money for us. Despite the unfortunate ending of our rental, we all agreed it was one of the most fun days of our lives together.

As a person that grew up around water, I've always loved being in or on the water. Pools, rivers, lakes, oceans… they all make me happy. The Vegas desert didn't have enough of those though. Lake Mead was about an hour from our apartment, and that rental experience didn't foretell any repeated events. Therefore, it was a regular occurrence that I would drink too much and start crying to Jason.

"Can we pleeeeeee-ase move back to the Northwest?" I asked, sobbing.

"No, honey," he said chuckling while rubbing my back in a half effort to console me.

"But whhhhhhhhy????" I brought this up sober as well, but when I drank too much, I felt the need to bring it up again. Yet by then it was too emotionally difficult to articulate, so I stuck to basic words. "Green! Blue! I mean, trees! Water! Family! Friends! Art museums! Culture! Liberalism and basic awareness!"

He laughed. "You're adorable. I like those things too, but our life is here. We have a great group of friends here, better than either of us have had before." Laughing to himself he said, "And strip clubs and smoking *and* drinking inside. Or smoking *and* drinking outside. Nice weather, pools, constant entertainment… You know it's more fun here, honey."

"But that's how *you* feel! I don't care about those things!" I whined.

"You don't care about our friends?" He asked, surprised.

I took a deep breath between sobs. "Okay, yes, I care about our friends. I love them. But I also love my friends back home!"

"Yeah, but didn't you say they never hang out all together as a group? You always have to make individual plans with them, right?"

"Well yeah, but I love them! We understand each other! We're liberal!"

That fall, I celebrated my birthday with my Vegas girlfriends, and I walked out on my own birthday dinner. The two women were first-generation Latina, and we were discussing the upcoming election between Barack Obama and Mitt Romney. They both told me they were voting for Romney because, "he is tough on borders and immigrants."

My jaw dropped. "But aren't you both first generation? I mean, your parents moved here to create better lives for you, right?"

"I mean, um, sure," Lisa said.

Missy chimed in, "Well, yeah, but we have too many people in this country. We don't need any more."

My mouth still agape, I asked, "So what if that was the law when your parents came here? You would be in Mexico, right? I mean, I love Mexico, but weren't your families barely surviving and that's why they moved?"

Lisa tried to explain, "Well, sure, but where's the limit? Do we let everyone in... Forever...?"

I tried my hardest not to roll my eyes at her ignorance and corrected, "This country doesn't just let everyone live here and the immigration process is nearly impossible for most people."

I had another Latina friend in Vegas, who was also first generation but didn't have legal papers because her mother never got them for her. She moved to the US when she was two, attended school here, and knew no other life but the one she had in the states. Yet when she researched her citizenship options, it proved impossible. It was easier for her to live off the grid. I loved her dearly. Missy and Lisa didn't feel the same way about her because she dated one of their exes, and they chose to maintain their preconceived notions, much like they did about politics.

I provided a brief explanation of the immigration laws, and then nearly yelled out of anger for their ignorance. "It's not even our land, anyway! The U.S. stole it from the Native Americans! Anyone should be allowed to live here! And anywhere they want! Why do we even have borders?!"

I stormed out of the restaurant and sat outside for 20 minutes while I recomposed myself. I eventually returned and we all agreed to stop talking about politics. Our conversation returned to its usual subjects —the men in our lives, shopping deals, our jobs, past and future group activities, and gossip.

So, when Jason mentioned our friends in Vegas as a selling point, to me it was equally a point of contention. They nicknamed me, "Hippie" because I did my best to ensure people recycled, and I was upset for months that our apartment building didn't have recycling. One day, I even drove our empty bottles and boxes 30 minutes across town to recycle them. I later reconciled with Jason's reasoning this wasted more time and gas than was worth it to recycle our refuse. It was only my concern for the environment which earned me that name. I barely spoke about politics or social justice since no one else wanted to discuss those issues. If they *did*, most friends held the conservative stance of leaving things how they were. But since they had such little awareness of "how things were," it was never much of a conversation. We could talk about politics with John and Anna, and some other work friends, but not with a majority of our close friends. And I still couldn't talk about it with his family.

On the other hand, I loved my friends and we always supported each other emotionally and professionally. We could always count on one another to lift us up, listen to our heartaches, and celebrate one another's birthdays with grandiose delight. We truly loved each other, but we just didn't talk about anything bigger than our little world.

I knew there was a bigger world out there, in which to travel and educate ourselves on others' lives and circumstances. I knew that my friends and family back home understood that, and more importantly actualized it. Yet Jason was more content than he'd ever been in our little circle. It was his life mission to continue that lifestyle, and to keep me a part of it.

So, our argument/my whining continued as a near-monthly pattern. The next time, I said, "Yes, I like it here, but I love it back home! Please, can we move back home?"

He laughed. "What is it this time, babe?"

"I miss nature!" I whined.

"There's trees and grass right outside! And a pool!"

"That's not what I mean," I pouted. "I need *real* trees and water." The landscaped trees in our apartment complex were barely a few years old, and the pool was not a natural water source.

He laughed again. I think this all amused him. "Those *are* real trees! Do you mean evergreens?"

I felt a little calmer once I knew he understood me. I took a deep breath and nodded.

He stroked my arm. "Okay, babe, we can go to Mount Charleston and Lake Mead more often. Will that make you happy?"

I nodded again, and then vehemently shook my head. "That would be nice, but it's not enough!" Mount Charleston is a large mountain an hour north of Vegas, but it's not visible from the city the way Mount Rainier and the Olympics are from the Northwest. Lake Mead is larger than Lake Washington, but it's surrounded by desert and to me it didn't have the same beauty as the latter.

Then he got more practical. "Could we even get jobs back home? We couldn't before we moved, so why do you think we would be able to now?"

"Well, the economy has gotten a lot better lately, under President Obama," I offered, and then suggested, "What if we got jobs at TravelCo Headquarters and convinced them to pay to move us back? It's their fault we live here in the first place; I bet we could talk them into it."

He laughed. "You're very optimistic. Sure, if that happens, I'll consider it."

I looked for jobs at headquarters every day for a month, and still found very little for which I was qualified. When I did find one, I told Jason about it. "Honey! This job sounds great! What do you think? Should I apply? If I do, and I get it, could we move?"

"Sure, you can apply. But what about me? Are there any jobs I could get?"

"I haven't found anything yet. Maybe you could finish your AA and then get a bachelor's degree? That would make you eligible for a lot more jobs."

"Yeah, I guess I could look into it... I don't know, though... I'm not sure how my credits would transfer here." He seemed sullen.

I became excited enough for both of us. "Let's look into it! You only have two classes left, right? I'm sure there's reciprocity programs!"

He patted me on the shoulder. "Okay, babe. I'll look into it."

Over the next few weeks, I asked him excitedly a few times, "Did you find anything out? Can you finish your AA here?"

He responded, "No, babe. It's a lot of work. Maybe later."

Then his answer eventually became, "I'll think about it, but I'm not ready to look into it at this point."

I finally stopped asking about school, but I still asked about moving home every month or so.

One day Jason got tired of the question, stood up, and firmly said, "*You* can go if you want. I'll be here. But you do what you want."

I tried once more, and he said the same thing but with more anger. The more frequently he responded that way, the less frequently I asked the question. I didn't want him to become angry, and I wanted to be part of his life more than anything. His love kept me happy more than any aspect of the Northwest and kept me on my life mission of "success." There was also a large part of me that enjoyed contentment, stability, and a life focused on love instead of paying attention to the news and all the misery of all that was wrong with the world.

Chapter 7 Warning Signs

This chapter shows a lot of the emotional abuse I endured. He called me names, he told me, "I couldn't do anything right," easily got angry and expected me to find solutions to make him happy, and "teased" me that "I don't have a sense of humor or know how to cook." Even though all these things are objectively horrible, I did not know what emotional abuse was at the time, so I did not know that was what it was. I thought that he was just a person that got angry often, and that sometimes he took it out on me. It may be also be a warning sign how easily he got angry. In a healthy relationship, people do experience anger, but not super frequently, and they do not take it out on their partner.

I tried to focus on the good times instead of the abuse. I even wrote, "As long as Jason was happy and not criticizing me, I didn't mind too much." This is a warning sign in that I ignored things that bothered me and turned that energy to what was going well. In a good relationship, people can communicate to one another about problems they have with each other.

I was happy that Jason had Clint to keep him happy, which made me feel less responsible for his happiness. I don't know why I felt responsible for his happiness, but I did. The few times I was able to make suggestions that he liked gave me motivation to continue trying, so I felt as though I had the ability to change his mood. In hindsight, I recognize that humans are not responsible for other human's moods. We can try and help, but we are not responsible for the outcomes of our assistance. In New Beginnings, the domestic violence advocacy group where I volunteered, we have a Bill of Rights. One of the rights says, "I am not responsible for other adult's problems." I know this now, but I did not at the time.

I was generally unhappy living in Las Vegas. I felt it was the complete opposite of living in Seattle – isolated from friends and family, in the desert, and in a different political climate. Jason never seemed to understand this or care that I didn't like living there. This is another example of his lack of empathy.

I was grateful that he eventually learned how to listen to me and support me through my work stress. However, once I taught him how to communicate about stresses, he took over the conversations and gave me less and less time to talk about my own stresses. This is another example of him being selfish, and taking control over our dynamic.

When Jason told Clint that he could hook up with Jenny if he wanted to, he showed another example of being patriarchal and sexist. Sexism is a warning sign in a heterosexual relationship because it shows that the abuser believes men should have power and privilege over women. He even said, "…I think she has a boyfriend, but I bet you could still get with her if you want." This statement shows that he did not care about

Jenny and her feelings, but simply saw her body as an objective for his friend. This showed a lack of respect for women, even his sister's best friend, which is sexism. I found it horrifying when he said it, but at the time I didn't translate his lack of respect of Jenny to his lack of respect for myself.

I ended the chapter with, "His love kept me happy more than any aspect of the Northwest and kept me on my life mission of 'success.'" Even though he was emotionally abusing me, disrespecting women, and disregarding my feelings about living in Las Vegas, I was still focused on my success goals and therefore still optimistic about the future Jason and I could have together. I had zero thoughts about leaving him through all of this. I was feeling emotionally dependent on him for love and support, and there were times he did give me that. Those times were the ones I held onto, the ones I focused on, and the ones that propelled me to move our relationship forward. That is the cycle of violence, shown here through emotional violence. Abusers bring their partners down through various forms of abuse, and then bring them back up again, which creates dependency and cravings for those good times, much like an addiction.

Chapter 8: Following

The next spring, in 2011, about a year and a half after we moved to Vegas, I asked Jason, "What are your thoughts for the future?"

Taken aback, and pausing from his usual jumpy nature, he stopped and squarely faced me. His voice heightened as he asked, "What do you mean? I like our routine! I don't think too much about the future."

But I thought about it a lot. I wanted more in life. I was shaking on the inside, but I replied as calmly as possible and said, "Well, when we first started dating, we talked about how we both want to get married, buy a house, and have kids. I'm about to turn 28 and I want to have kids before I'm 30..."

He sat down. He seemed to be mentally preparing himself to focus on the conversation. I followed his lead and sat down next to him. I slowly breathed in the faint scent of jasmine flowers in the distance. I tried to remain calm, but instead I spoke as though I was running a marathon. "Well, I want to be married for at least two years before we have kids so we can feel really comfortable being married first. And I want to buy a house after we get married, so ideally, we would do that within our first year of marriage so we can get through the home buying process and get used to being homeowners and have a nice house in a good neighborhood where we can raise our kids." When I get excited, nervous, or both, I speak in quick run-on sentences. I worry the other person might try and shut down my ideas before hearing my complete thought, so I try and get it out as quickly as I can. My parents taught me to always defend my thoughts and actions, to prove I knew who I was and that I was making conscious decisions. I always felt I needed to prove myself to Jason, but not because he wanted me to make good choices but because he always wanted to prove that he was right and made better decisions than I did. He stared at me blankly while I tried to process my words.

I smiled broadly and continued, "So if we get engaged within the next year, I think we can achieve this plan. What do you think? Do you like this plan?"

He leaned his head back and exhaled. "Woah. That's a lot to take in." He angled his body away from me and looked away.

"I know," I gently replied with a small pout. I wanted to stroke his arm to calm him down, but I could tell he needed space. We had similar conversations before, so I knew it would be okay, yet it was the first time we really talked about everything concretely with a timeline in mind, and I could tell he was uncomfortable. I felt guilty for overwhelming him. I focused on breathing steadily and staying strong. These successful life "steps" had been on my mind for years, and I finally felt ready to get them off my chest and make them happen. I was happy to fully open myself to my boyfriend I loved. I knew he just needed a minute to process everything. I reminded myself of all this while I attempted to patiently wait for his response.

After a few moments, he turned his body toward me and calmly looked at me. "Well, it makes sense. But do we really need to be married two whole years before we have kids?"

"Yes," I persisted, speaking excitedly in run-on sentences again. "My mom always said she recommends waiting two years before having children, as that's what she did, and even that wasn't a long enough time because she and my dad still ended up getting divorced. But she has always insisted that she is happy she had my sister and I, and she doesn't regret it. Even so, she recommends waiting two years before having kids, and then being engaged for at least a year before getting married, and I think that makes sense."

Defensively whining he responded, "But, your parents got divorced! Mine are still together and they didn't wait that long before getting married or having kids. Maybe we can revisit this conversation in a few months?" He basically suggested we wait to get engaged and then shorten the timeline of having children.

Gently, I responded, "I know. It sounds like we are saying we want the same thing but at difference paces. But don't you think it makes more sense to wait before each big life decision? At the same time, though, I feel like I'm ready to get this ball rolling, because I'm already

28 and at this rate I'll still be past my goal of kids before 30."

"Hmm...I see..." he said, pouting. He took a deep breath, and then his eyes glimmered, and a smile spread on his face. "Well, yeah, that does make sense. Okay, yeah... I guess I haven't thought about the future too much. But I want kids before I'm 30 too, and with this plan it will be before I'm 30. But ha! You'll be 31!" He teased me, as he often did.

I laughed and agreed, and we hugged each other closely and kissed. We were ready to start our lives together.

Chapter 8 Warning Signs

The main issue in this chapter is that I pushed our relationship forward, even though it was clear he was telling me he wasn't ready. I was so determined to keep my life plan on track, that I continued moving forward without giving it much thought if it was the right relationship or time for us.

A more minor warning sign is that he made me feel I had to prove myself. In a healthy relationship, partners support each other and accept each other without judgment. No one needs to prove themselves to the other because both people accept each other. Jason, on the other hand, always seemed as though he was proving to me that he was right about everything, even when they were generally just a matter of differing opinions, such as what movie to watch.

I also wrote that I felt guilty for overwhelming him, but I was really just attempting to have a mature conversation about making plans for the future. People should not have to feel guilty for bringing up difficult conversation topics, no matter how difficult.

He teased me about my age in this conversation, which is not necessarily a warning sign, because gentle teasing happens in healthy relationships too. What makes it more difficult to determine whether or not this was a warning sign, is that he emotionally abused me in the form of "jokes" so it was hard to tell the difference. I think to determine whether or not the "jokes" or "teasing" are indeed those, or are emotional abuse, is how the words make you feel. If you are genuinely laughing along with them, then I think it counts as teasing. If you are not, and your instincts tell you something is wrong, then it is emotional abuse.

Chapter 9: Betrothing

Summer in Vegas was harsh. The mornings were 90 degrees and the afternoons reached 110 to 115. There wasn't much wind or cloud cover, so the nights stayed hot. I was miserable, though I took solace in having so many fun things to do in cool, air-conditioned casinos. We saw live music, Elvis-impersonation shows, comedians, burlesque, and everything in between. We delighted in the endless entertainment options.

One night we went out to see a late 80s rock cover band with our friends, and we got back in our car around midnight. The car temperature gauge read 107. Midnight and 107? The heat felt inescapable. There was no time of day that offered reprieve. 107 degrees at midnight felt like Vegas was mocking us, saying, "You chose to live here! Ha! Can you handle it?"

My sister, Kristina, graduated college the same week as her birthday that year, so I went home to celebrate with her. I knew Jason and I would get engaged soon, so prior to the trip he and I talked about wedding ideas so that I could start making plans while I was there. I only visited once every six months, on average, which meant I wouldn't be back again until after we got engaged. I needed to make the most out of my time in Seattle.

Would we get married outside or inside? What time of year? What kind of venue ideas did we like? Seattle or Vegas? We agreed it made sense to host the wedding in

Seattle because our family lived there, and it would have been more expensive to ask everyone to fly to us in Vegas. I had always wanted an outside wedding, but he made a pretty logical argument about the weather's unpredictability. Therefore, we considered inside wedding venues, and he agreed to my idea of an art gallery or museum.

Before the trip I researched options and created a map of all the potential galleries and museums. When I arrived, I scouted all the venues with Kristina and my friends. Then I narrowed the list down from 35 to 10 potential options to discuss with Jason. I loved researching everything to ensure we made the best choices, and he hated planning and having too many options. I really wanted to make every decision together, but he said that even 10 felt like too many options for him. This seemed reasonable to me compared to the infinite possibilities, so I saw it as our version of a compromise.

I also met with his family while back home. His mom, dad, and sisters met me in Seattle, where they infrequently traveled, despite being less than an hour from their house. I appreciated them coming to meet me, and to show them this appreciation I showed them one of my favorite places in Seattle. We met in Pioneer Square, a historic neighborhood of concrete buildings and cobblestone streets, where there is a hidden waterfall. I lived in the city for years before I knew about its existence, and when I found it it, I felt like I found a hidden gem. Water gushed from large slate rocks, magenta rhododendrons bloomed, and birds sang. His family said they loved it as much as I did, so it was the perfect setting for our meeting.

Jason had been previously engaged and had bought his fiancée a diamond ring. When the engagement ended, he procured the ring back and his parents kept it safe.

We weren't just meeting to enjoy the waterfall, but to pass the ring from them to me. It felt strange to receive a ring originally purchased for someone else, but it also felt wasteful to spend money on another ring when we already had one, not that we had any to spare anyhow. Cassie presented the ring to me. She grinned and held it out to me, almost as though she was proposing herself. I felt like his family was including me in their lives just as much as he did, and I felt honored.

The ring was visibly flawless. It sparkled and bounced light from the magenta rhododendrons to the water droplets hanging in the sky. We smiled brightly with excitement about the new life their son and I would be creating.

I flew back to Vegas a few days later and returned the ring to its temporary owner. Jason asked, "Are you sure this isn't weird for you?"

"Well, it is a little. But also, the ring is too small for my fingers so we can get it reset and then it will feel like it's a new ring just for us."

He chuckled, "Yeah, her fingers are smaller than yours. Yours are kind of fat."

It felt unnecessary for him to tease me in what should have been a romantic moment, but that was his communication style, and I was used to it. I playfully shoved a pillow towards him and laughed. "Alright, we'll get a setting that fits my fat fingers."

A few months later, when he felt ready, we went to jewelry stores and looked at our options. I had been ready for this moment since I retrieved the ring; I was jumping for joy that it seemed he had finally met me in the same emotional place.

We went to a few stores. Most of them firmly told us a new gold setting would cost nearly $1,000. That was a lot more money than we had to spend on a ring. The sun was setting, and stores were closing, so we went home without a decision, feeling disappointed.

When we got home, I went online and researched our options, determined to find a setting we could afford. He asked me to put the computer away and relax with him, but I didn't want to end our night without a solution.

I found a store nearby that offered free quotes and custom designs, and I went to talk to them later that week. I looked at the options, brought in old jewelry for trade, and got an estimate that we could afford! I was beyond elated and knew Jason would be happy he didn't have to do the research work he hated so much.

"Oh, so you went to the ring store and chose your own engagement ring without me?" he asked, playfully teasing me.

"Well, yeah, I just made it easier for you!" I eagerly showed him the design, continuing, "And it's not too expensive! We can afford this, and it will be beautiful! You can pick it up at the end of the week!"

He gently grumbled under his breath, before he stepped back and smiled. He stepped forward and said, "Thank you; you did make this really easy for me and I appreciate that." We kissed and tightly embraced, excited for our future together.

Later that week the jewelry store called saying the ring was ready, and I texted Jason to let him know. He replied, "LOL I'm not sure this is how this usually works but okay. I'll pick it up."

That night he told me he got it, but he would propose when he was ready. I understood and did my best to contain my excitement. I put all my nervous energy into cleaning the apartment and preparing our home for our new life together. He sat on the couch, watched TV, and played on his phone.

He called over to me, and asked, "Θα με παντρευτείς?"

"What?" I asked, laughing. "You know I don't know Greek!"

He laughed back. "Yeah, I know, I've been asking you to learn it with me! You said you would, but you never did." He let out a loud belly laugh and teased me. "If you had learned it then you would know what I said! You'll have to figure it out!"

I joined him on the couch and excitedly opened the computer to a translation website. I had a feeling what he meant, but he remained steadfast, and didn't give me any clues while he watched me. I repeated the pronunciation and tried several unsuccessful attempts at entering my understanding into the website. I enjoyed the challenge and had fun solving a puzzle, but I was also struggling. I also didn't want to be presumptuous; I really wanted to understand what he said.

Eventually he wrote it out in the Greek alphabet. He taught me a few letters a few months prior, though not all of them. He patiently, but excitedly, taught me each letter in the phrase, and helped me sound it out to determine each word.

"Know?" I guessed because the letters seemed close to that, even though I was pretty sure what the real question was.

He shook his head and laughed. "No, but it is a question! You're on the right track!"

"What?" I asked to hide my ability to guess, much like I did when I asked him how to "save as" on the computer.

He shook his head, "No." "Keep trying!" He beamed.

"Will?"

He sat straight up and beamed with delight. "Yes! Can you figure out the next word?"

"You?" I smiled back. I raised one eyebrow to show him intrigue and excitement, yet also try to feign confusion to placate him.

"Yes!" He exclaimed, as he jumped off the couch.

I jumped up to join him. He retrieved the ring from the bag and presented it to me with a grin. A thin, white gold band held a solitaire round diamond set in a slightly raised square setting, giving the appearance of being a larger emerald cut diamond. It was perfect. "Θα με παντρευτείς?" he asked again.

"Yes!" I shrieked with joy and jumped two feet in the air. We hugged and kissed while we jumped around our living room, relishing our moment of our lives officially beginning together. We both called our families and close friends to tell them the good news. After, he said he didn't want to do anything to celebrate, but I begged him and then he let us go to my favorite restaurant to celebrate with champagne.

Chapter 9 Warning Signs

In this chapter I also did everything to propel our relationship forward, as I had become increasingly dependent upon him to fulfill my success goals. I researched wedding venues, I picked up the ring from his family, found a ring setting, and had it made. I did all but propose. I was not very patient at this time in my life.

There was emotional abuse when he called my fingers fat. What made this particularly bad is that he said it at a time when I was feeling especially vulnerable to him and we were talking about our engagement, our future together. I was so enamored that we were actually about to get engaged, though, so I ignored it. And I was feeling so vulnerable and close to him, that I chose to hang onto that feeling of it being a good time instead of pay attention to how his words made me feel.

It was a bit of a warning sign that I pretended to not know what the Greek words were, even once I had figured it out. People should not have to pretend that they are not smart, or that they don't know something, just to make the other person feel better. In a healthy relationship, people appreciate one another's intelligence.

The major warning signs in this chapter are that I wrote about how much I compromised with Jason, since I didn't realize how emotionally dependent upon him I had become. I had always wanted an outdoor wedding, but he made me feel that was not a reasonable option. Seattle weather is not perfect, but it is fairly predictable in its seasons. We easily could have planned a summer wedding with limited chance of anything more than light rain.

When we did finally get engaged, I had to beg him to let us go out and celebrate. I thought it was weird that he didn't want to do anything to celebrate, even though it was such a pivotal and romantic time in our lives. So, I took it as that him compromising with me to go out and celebrate. But, again, I was feeling enamored and vulnerable, and I was focusing on the good time we were having. I loved that he proposed to me in another language and that he made it a puzzle for me to solve with him. I thought that part of it was fun and romantic, so I focused on that feeling. At the time, these decisions did feel like equal compromises, so I felt that everything was fine. I had yet to realize how much of the time I was making compromises while he was getting his way.

Chapter 10: Planning

Fall in Vegas was spectacular. The few older trees that were around became bright red and orange, which was a welcome addition of color to the desert scene with young green trees lining every street. It was still hot. Not quite as hot as the penetrating summers, but seemingly more manageable, with the optimism of the end of insufferable heat just around the corner. We spent fall evenings hanging out at friends' backyards and patio bars, soaking up the gentle 90-degree sun. Clint had been laid off from his job that fall, so he and Jenny moved back home to the Northwest. Jason and I were sad, and we became even more grateful for our Las Vegas friends.

Our two close friends, Missy, who attended my birthday dinner, and Chris, got married that fall. They had a beautiful outdoor golf course ceremony and a seated four-course dinner reception. Jason and I observed what we liked and didn't like and found inspiration for our own wedding plans. We loved that they choose individual songs for each group of people in the procession, suited to the couple's taste, and we loved the simple floral arrangements. We hated that after the ceremony the couple had their photos taken and we had to wait for them while we sat at the same table that we were relegated to all night. We compared mental notes and were pleased we shared the same opinions about how we would plan our wedding. Since we agreed on most everything, Jason said he trusted me to plan our wedding.

The art museums and galleries all ended up being too expensive once we factored in table and chair rentals, and catering. Instead, we found a beautiful hotel that featured artwork and books on its walls, that already had tables and chairs, and a caterer. It was perfect. Then, over the next eight months, I spent countless nights researching myriad options. I looked at hundreds of wedding photography websites and narrowed it down to a few photographer choices. I also did this with flowers, decorations, and every other aspect of the wedding. Then I presented the options to Jason for us to decide together, just like I did with the venues. I enjoyed all the research, but also found it took a *lot* of time. On work breaks I called vendors and at night I relayed my findings to Jason. I was constantly thinking about the wedding and what decisions needed to be made. Each time we narrowed something down or decided something it seemed like another impending decision came forward.

One day I asked him if we could look at wedding decoration ideas, and he said he was tired of talking about the wedding. He made me agree to only ask him about it one day of the week. He even added a tab to my one gigabyte Wedding Excel Sheet. The tab title was, "Can we talk about the wedding today?" The Excel formula output was, "Enter the day of the week and if the day is Sunday the formula says, 'Yes'." "If the day is any other day, the answer is, 'No'." I chuckled; I was amused and impressed about his solution. On the inside, though, I felt alone in planning *our* wedding. He felt we needed more balance in our lives, and I felt he didn't understand how much work went into planning the perfect wedding. His idea of balance was working and relaxing. It never seemed to include planning for the future in any way.

This frustrated me, but I kept chugging ahead with the research while he grew frustrated, I wasn't "relaxing" with him and focusing more on our TV shows. He told me multiple times he was fine with anything I chose, and I appreciated that he trusted me. One time, I went to California to visit family and stopped by Ikea to buy wedding decorations. I chose simple, clear, square vases to hold roses and candles. When I came home, he said he didn't like anything I bought. He said then, but not earlier, that he had wanted round vases. I liked the square ones because they were more modern, but he said he didn't care and that they were ugly. I almost returned everything because he seemed so mad about it, but eventually he let me keep them since he knew it was more hassle than it was worth to try and ship back 25 vases to the store. More importantly, though, I stressed how important it was that we made decisions together – I didn't want this to be *my* wedding; I wanted it to be *our* wedding. So, I did my research and patiently waited for his Sunday Wedding Opinions.

I also wanted him to take care of, and have more say in, some aspects, so I asked him to choose the music and honeymoon. He agreed. He listened to music more often than I did, as I preferred listening to the news, and he still worked in leisure travel. We both understood these were aspects he would enjoy and where his knowledge reigned. It was March 2012, just three months prior to our wedding date, though, and he still hadn't made any decisions. We spent one evening talking about music and listening to different style ideas. It was the most fun we had together in a while. It really felt like we were bonding and being equally invested in our wedding. We chose several songs, and I chose the remaining ones later that week.

The next week we planned the honeymoon. He really wanted to go back to Greece, so he insisted we were going there. I reminded him that there's so much more of the world to see, and it would be good for him to see and experience more. I also told him I had always wanted to go to France, so I suggested a trip that included both countries. He complained that would cost more money and take more time. I told him I wasn't going to Europe without seeing at least one part of France. He told me he wasn't going if he couldn't see at least one of the islands in Greece. We were both frustrated. I checked prices on a few trip options and realized we didn't have enough money for both, let alone any country in Europe.

I said to Jason, "So, we can't afford Europe…" I looked up a few major Asian cities, then the rest of the continents. I pouted. "Well, we can't afford any cities outside of North America; not even Central America."

He laughed. "So… we've narrowed it down to North America?"

We cracked up. We knew there were innumerable choices inside North America.

We talked about domestic ideas such as New Orleans or New York, but they didn't feel fancy enough. We looked at options in Mexico, but he insisted then we had to go to an all-inclusive resort. I had no interest in an all-inclusive vacation, as I relished experiencing food and dining as part of the culture.

We finally settled on the Caribbean! Neither of us had ever been and we were excited. We could afford it, we got time to lay on the beach, and we got to explore a new culture. It checked all the boxes for both of us. We spent the next few weeks researching the islands and comparing their benefits. We chose an island and booked our trip.

Planning the wedding was difficult and stressful, yet ultimately a fun learning experience. We, well mostly I, created the perfect wedding for us. After the wedding my dad told me, "You know how to throw one hell of a party!"

Chapter 10 Warning Signs

The amount of compromises I made with Jason become clearer here. He told me he trusted me to plan the wedding, so I did plan most of it, but I also felt he said that to manipulate me to do all the work. I tried to make decisions with him early on, but he grew easily frustrated and he eventually made the Excel sheet to tell me he would only discuss it one day of the week.

I saw that he was trying to help by telling me to relax, but here was so much to do that I felt I couldn't do it all alone. I also didn't want to do it alone because it was *our* wedding. I shouldn't have felt alone in planning our wedding. In a healthy relationship, people make decisions together and do their best to put in an equal amount of work.

In healthy relationships, people also don't tell people when they can and cannot bring up important conversation topics. They do set boundaries, though, which he was doing. In this situation, it was a very fine line between him setting a boundary of when he would allow the conversation topic and not allowing me to have conversations with him.

It is perfectly acceptable for him to have set boundaries. The reason this became a problem, though, is that I did not set my own boundaries so I unknowingly allowed him to hurt and control me. When one person vies for control, and the other person does not set their boundaries about what they will and will not accept, then the person vying for control can gain more and more control of the other person.

If I had set my own boundaries of what behavior and communication I would and would not allow, I would have recognized when he crossed them and said something. Then, if I said something and he did not respect my boundary, then perhaps I would have ended the relationship.

At this time in my life, though, I did not know what boundaries were, so I did not know where to set them. This is the crux of this book. If people know what the warning signs of abuse are, then they will know where to set their boundaries, and prevent the abuse from occurring or leave when it does. If I had recognized that all Jason's "teasing" and putting me down was actually emotional abuse, and if I had set a boundary around myself not to allow that, then I might have stopped it from happening or left him.

I picture a boundary like a hula hoop around myself. The hula hoop spins around me, creating a space between me and another person. I can hula hoop with another person, nearby, and even touching one another, but the other person would also still be spinning their hula hoop around themselves, creating their own space and energy. If either of us touched one another's hula hoop, then it would stop it from spinning and crash to the ground, thereby eliminating the boundary of the hula hoop.

This is not to say that we do not allow people to enter our spaces in healthy relationships, including non-romantic relationships. It is to say that even when we do allow someone into our space, people that respect us will respect our boundaries. I can allow people to come into the hula hoop area with me, but only if I choose to move the hula hoop up or down to allow them to step through. This person would then be inside my bubble, but they would not have broken the actual hula hoop. If someone disrespects a boundary, then that person does not respect the person with the boundaries, and has a greater likelihood of controlling and/or abusing that person. I recommend making a list for yourself, or use this list of warning signs at the back of each book, as a bare minimum set of boundaries.

When I did ask Jason for input on wedding decisions, he didn't fairly communicate with me – he insisted we did things his way. He insisted we would go to Greece, he insisted we would go to an all-inclusive resort, and he insisted I returned the vases he thought were "ugly." Thankfully, I spoke up and he did not win any of those points, but that does not change how his insistance made me feel. I felt emotionally invaded, because he was trying to cross my boundaries.

This can also be viewed from the power and control wheel, where it says, "Using Male Privilege." Jason acted like the "master of the castle," by insisting we would do things his way or not at all. He said he would only go to Mexico if we went to an all-inclusive resort, so we did not go to Mexico. The Caribbean ended up being great, and at the time it felt as though we made equal compromises to arrive at that decision but looking back, I compromised more than he did.

I tried to give him the feeling of being in control in the areas that I thought he would enjoy, such as planning the music and the honeymoon. But, when he hadn't started working on either of those three months before the wedding, I knew I had to step in to get things done. At the time, I saw it as him being lazy. Now I see it as him purposely not doing anything as a way to manipulate me to do it all myself, which is also a warning sign. I not only compromised on the decisions I was making with him, but I heavily compromised in the amount of planning work I thought I was signing up for. Feeling that the relationship is one-sided, and not in an equal partnership, is a definite warning sign for the relationship to be continue being unequal moving forward.

Chapter 11: Wedding

I spent so much time planning the wedding, and was so invested in its theoretical impending perfection, that I was a nervous wreck the days prior. I spent upwards of 1,000 hours working on this wedding and I did everything in my power to make it perfect. I even designed our own logo to use on our invitations, napkins, and shot glass souvenirs. I found this adorable picture of Jason hugging and kissing me, so I traced the outline of us and turned it into our logo.

I arrived in Seattle a few days before the wedding to finalize preparations and enjoy the beautiful weather in May. The wedding roses arrived at my mom's house in Seattle two nights before the wedding. They were beautiful, but they were still tight buds and hadn't bloomed open yet. I cried to my mom, "But! I pictured big, beautiful roses floating in big square vases! Should we open each petal individually? That won't look good, though, right? Or be good for the flowers?"

My mom put her arm around me and said, "It's okay, honey. We'll put them in the pantry where it's nice and warm and by tomorrow they'll open more."

My cries turned to those of thankfulness, and I hugged her. "Thank you, Mom!"

The next day the roses opened to half blooms. It was enough to make me happy. Later that night, my mom, Kristina, and friend Lisa arranged the bouquets and prepared the roses for their vases. They were bright magenta roses with silky cream outlines. They reminded me of my favorite roses my grandma used to grow in her backyard. I loved them.

As we began arranging the bouquets, we realized it was more difficult than we realized to "simply" group a bunch of roses with a ribbon. The flowers didn't lay just right, the tape was so sticky it was difficult to work with, and my family and I didn't seem to have the dexterity needed to work with the roses and tape at once. We sighed to each other in desperation.

I cried, "How are we going to do this?! I can't do it! Why is this so much harder than I thought it would be?" The tiniest things stressed me out. I wanted Jason's emotional support, but I didn't want to bother his short time with his family and friends. We were only back home for a few days before the wedding, and the day after the wedding we planned to leave for our honeymoon.

Lisa rubbed my shoulder, smiled a knowing smile, and chuckled as she said, "It's okay, honey. It is a lot harder than it looks. But I used to help at my sister-in-law's florist shop, so I can do the bouquets for you guys. Do you want to work on the boutonnieres? All you need to do is cut the stems and stick pins through them."

We all laughed and said, "Yes, we can do that! Thank you so much!"

Chapter 11: Wedding

Lisa's knowledge and initiative re-inspired my positivity for the wedding. I felt all would be right in the world. Wedding planning definitely hit the clichéd mark of an emotional rollercoaster.

I planned for the bridal party, my sister and Jason's two sisters, to get our nails done and have brunch the morning of the wedding. I was looking forward to bonding with everyone. But at the last minute, Jason's two sisters told me they wouldn't be able to make it. Kristina was the third bridesmaid, the maid of honor, and she was wonderfully by my side the entire process. The rest of us had a great afternoon, but I didn't appreciate the extra dip on the rollercoaster. I proceeded to my hair appointment, which was a wedding gift from a close hairdresser friend.

When I returned to the hotel, Jason's sisters had said they would be there to get ready together, but they texted that they were stuck in traffic. It was still a pleasant day, even though I got anxious during lunch, and it was not going as smoothly as I wanted. My wedding day jitters were in full force.

His sisters finally arrived and quickly got ready with us. I planned to be ready half an hour prior to the wedding to set table decorations with my mom and some friends, but when that time arrived, I wasn't ready. I got stressed again. I cried to my Mom, "How are we going to get this all done? People are already arriving!"

As gently as she typically speaks, she said, "It's okay, honey. We will find a way to take care of everything. You just focus on relaxing and enjoying your wedding day."

I dropped my shoulders and smiled. "Thank you, Mom. Okay, I'll try."

Kristina encouraged me too. "Yeah! Just have fun! Don't worry about anything!"

I grimaced to myself and smiled on the outside. "Okay, thank you both."

What felt like only moments later, my mom burst through the door exclaiming, "Your friends and I set up everything and it all looks perfect! Here! I took a picture to show you! Do you like it? We had a couple choices, and we went with this one."

I felt tears well in my eyes. "Ohhh... It *is* perfect. Thank you so much! I love you so much!"

She wrapped her arms around me, and I tried not to cry. My Mom and Kristina's support and optimism carried me through the day.

The photographers arrived and took pictures of us getting ready and putting wedding jewelry on one another. Then we took the elevator down to greet the guests and photograph the time Jason and I first saw each other in our suit and gown.

My breath was shallow, and my hands were shaking. I couldn't believe I was about to get married. A thousand thoughts flew through my head, racing between wondering if I was making the right decision, if it was too late to decide otherwise now, and grandiose emotions of how much I loved him. I took several deep breaths, rolled back my shoulders, and stepped out of the elevator in my ivory Vera Wang dress and sparkling fuchsia heels, and stepped into my new life.

I walked through the lobby and said hello to my friends and family. Someone called out, "There's Jason!" I spun around, searching for his face in the sea of people. I noticed it was strange I didn't immediately identify my soon-to-be-husband in a crowd of people. With other men I had dated I was able to find them right away, no matter the size of the crowd. I chalked it up to stress and reveled in his delight to see me.

"Hi!" He excitedly greeted me with a grin. He looked so adorable in his suit and silver tie we chose together. We embraced and kissed, while everyone around us watched and applauded. I was still nervous, but his embrace relaxed me, and I felt much more joyous than I had the rest of the day. I finally saw my almost-husband, and all my beautifying preparations paid off – he seemed ecstatic to see me.

We greeted our wedding guests and took pictures with our families. Then the bridal party and I stepped outside so we could formally enter the ceremony. Our venue, a hotel with art on its walls, had a grand staircase leading up to our altar, which was a sunlit landing. The crowd gathered on the steps and anxiously awaited our entrance. It was a beautiful spring day, and we counted ourselves lucky to see the sun shining in Seattle; despite rain being a good omen for weddings.

The theme song from *The Hangover* played, which is a movie about a group of groomsmen partying the night before a wedding, and the groomsmen joyfully walked up, most likely with the same eponymous feeling.

Then, "The Imperial March", the Darth Vader theme song from *Star Wars* began, and Jason excitedly hopped up the stairs. When he initially told me that's what he wanted to play I thought he was joking. I cracked up.

He laughed back. "What, babe?" he said, kissing me on the cheek. And then, excitedly, "You know how much I love *Star Wars*! Oh, and wait, didn't you say you haven't seen all the movies?"

"I've seen the original ones, and that's enough for me," I said flatly.

"Do you even know which numbers those are?" he playfully teased me.

I rolled my eyes at him. "Yes, the original ones are 4 through 7. I get it."

He laughed even harder. "But you haven't seen the rest! You don't even know the backstory!"

I rolled my eyes harder. "I get it. Darth Vader was Luke's father. Space and stuff. I'm good."

We both cracked up, and then he said, "Okay, well you don't really know. You have to watch all of the *Star Wars* movies and all of *The Godfather* movies before we get married. Oh, and! And *The Sopranos*! It's soooo good!"

I rolled my eyes while laughing. "Or else we're not getting married? Are you for real?"

He laughed again. "Yeah! That's all I need!"

I shook my head and said, "Okay, well I need you to do dishes when I cook. Or cook. Your choice. I'll watch some stupid movies and TV shows with you if you'll help me more around the house."

He whined, "They're not stupid! You'll love them!"

I laughed and narrowed my eyes. "Doubtful. But you agree to help around the house more if I watch your shows?"

He squared off to face me directly and said, "Yes."

I smiled broadly and stuck out my hand. "Shake on it?"

He smiled broadly and shook my hand. "Deal!"

We kissed to seal the deal, and I begrudgingly followed up on my end of the agreement. It turned out I did *not* love the movies, nor did he hold up his end.

Next, "Girls, Girls, Girls" by Motley Crue played and cued the bridesmaids. Kristina turned to looked at me, and noticed my raised eyebrows and wide eyes showing obvious anxiety. She gave me a big hug and encouragingly said, "This will be great!" I thanked her and watched her and Jason's sisters dance up the aisle.

"Are You Gonna Be My Girl" by Jet began playing, and I greeted my father with a hug. He took my hand and we danced and spun up the aisle together. We kissed each other's cheeks at the top, then he shook Jason's hand and stepped aside.

There we were, at the top of the stairs, about to take the plunge. Jason and I grinned at each other as my stepdad, Hal, began officiating. I planned our ceremony to a T. Dotted every "i" and crossed every "t." I planned what Hal would say, what I would say, the fact that the first dance would happen at exactly 5:45… I planned it all. Hal read my introduction, and then I read my vows. I had taken the time to write heartfelt vows. I told Jason how much I loved him and how excited I was to marry him and noticed a few tears stream down my cheek as I grinned. I spoke for several minutes about how Jason made me feel. I described his love, his warmth, and everything I loved about him.

Jason read his vows next. "I've loved you in the past, I love you now, and I'll always love you."

I felt tears run down my cheeks. Not because they were so sweet, but because they weren't. They didn't seem like his words, and he read them in a monotone voice with a half-smile as he finished.

A few days prior, he had called me and asked, "Do we really have to write our own vows?"

I sighed. "Yeah, I would really like it if we did. I want our wedding to be personal, and about us."

"Oh, okay," he sighed back. "Well, I found this poem about past, present, and future love, and I liked it, so I think I'll just use that." He laughed heartily.

I cringed. "Honey, please use your own words and feelings. We're marrying each other because we love each other, right? Can you please use your own words to describe how you feel about me? "

He laughed back, "Sure, honey, I was just kidding. Of course, I can do that."

But he didn't. He read what he found online instead of writing with his own voice. I suddenly felt a flood of emotions, like the ones people say they feel before they die. But I wasn't dying, I was getting married. I felt all my prior emotions about wedding planning flash in front of me. I thought about my one gigabyte Excel sheet, all my work break time and evenings used for wedding planning, and all the hours he spent playing on his phone while I fussed over every detail. I poured all my heart and soul into this marriage and this wedding, and all he could muster was a synopsis of something someone else wrote. I was devastated. I turned to the crowd and saw all our friends and family, anxiously awaiting us to seal the deal and share our first kiss as a married couple. Seeing their faces made me smile.

Hal joyfully exclaimed, "You may kiss each other!" I was careful in my wedding planning to express gender equity.

Jason grinned, threw open his arms, and kissed me like no one was watching. Except everyone was watching. We kissed, and kissed, and kissed, and eventually stopped to grin at each other. He held out his hand, and I grabbed it as we galloped down the ceremony stairs. Our wedding guests showered us with rose petals, and "A Little Less Conversation" by Elvis played on the sound system. We exited the building and turned to excitedly kiss each other.

"We did it!" he exclaimed with a sloppy kiss on my cheek.

I squinted through tears, while smiling. "Yes! I can't believe it!"

"It's real!" he responded with glee. We embraced and kissed and returned to our wedding guests cheering for us. We heard "Howling for You" by the Black Keys play as we entered our wedding reception. I felt happy to be married to the man I loved, and happy to feel his joy.

Our wedding was beautiful. The single pink roses floated in square vases on each table just as I wanted. It was simple, elegant, and perfect. Our cake was a three-tiered ivory cake with black ribbon swirls and actual black ribbon lining the bottom of each tier. We had a food spread of oysters, crab cakes, grilled vegetables, bruschetta, and sliders, practically overflowing. Wedding guests mingled and dined as they pleased, without any timing or seated constrictions. They drank wine and our favorite local Seattle beer, Mack and Jack's, as well as a craft cocktail I concocted with champagne, vodka, St. Germaine elderflower liqueur, and fresh raspberries. I named it the "Jate" as our friends called us, for Jason and Kate.

Since neither Jason nor I were dancers, we chose an upbeat song that would allow us to be cheesy and have fun: Chuck Berry's "You Never Can Tell." He had also said he didn't want a sappy, romantic slow dance, even though it was our wedding dance. He convinced me it would be more fun to have a silly dance. My father and I danced to The Temptations' "My Girl," and Jason and his mom danced to a country song about love. The DJ cued up "Rock and Roll All Night" by Kiss to signal to the guests that it was time to party! We danced and drank and had a fantastic time. It was so great to spend time with my Seattle friends, aunts, and uncles, all of whom I loved dearly yet saw less than twice per year.

For the garter toss, Jason chose "Pour Some Sugar on Me" by Def Leppard. I originally chose it for the bouquet toss but he said it was such a common song to hear in strip clubs that it would make more sense for it to be his song, since he is the "man." I smirked and obliged, and instead chose Robert Palmer's "Addicted to Love." Perhaps I was addicted to his love. It brought me to Las Vegas and kept me there, after all.

By cake cutting time, Jason and I were both pretty drunk and having fun with our friends and family. Jason's immediate had family left earlier, citing his mother not feeling well. I was surprised and saddened to hear they left without saying goodbye to me. Cassie once told me she noticed that in her experience, that "only weddings with good cakes had marriages that survived." Yet she didn't wait to taste our cake.

Although, she may have waited awhile. Our guests had to come find us to tell us we needed to cut the cake because our older guests were ready to leave. We were immersed in spending time with our friends we rarely got to see. The DJ played "I Want to Love You Madly" by Cake, and we held the knife and cut the cake together. Beforehand we agreed we would not shove the cake in one another's faces, so I felt relaxed about the cake portion of our wedding. However, Jason, being the prankster he is, grabbed a handful of cake with his hands and flung it towards my face. My eyes widened as Jason's smile broke out into a teasing grin. "I told you I wouldn't do that, babe! Don't you trust me?" he laughed. I narrowed my eyes at him, as I wondered if I did trust him, and he put the cake back on the plate. I joined him in laughter as we fed each other a bite of cake.

Then we returned to drinking and having fun with our wedding guests. Once our venue rental time ended, several of us still wanted to party so we went to an Irish bar next door and danced to the live band. Jason didn't dance, but I wanted to, so I took turns dancing with a few male friends. I think he was too drunk to be jealous. He usually got jealous when I called my male friends on the phone to catch up, let alone danced with them.

We celebrated, as he exclaimed, "We pulled it off! We got married!" We all took shots and cheered in celebration. After the bar closed, Jason and I finally went to our honeymoon suite.

Jason was eager to consummate the marriage, but I was exhausted. Slowly, and most likely slurring some words, I said to him, "Can we please just lay down and sleep? I've been planning this wedding for six months, and now that it's done, I can finally relax, and all I want to do is sleep."

Angered, turning red, he yelled, "No! Are you kidding me? Are you fucking kidding me right now? This is our wedding night!"

Shocked and still so tired, I said, "No, I'm not kidding. I know and I'm sorry but I'm so tired. Maybe if you had helped me more with the research and planning, you would have felt as invested in it and you would be exhausted too."

He jumped back, aghast. "But this is our wedding night! You are my wife! You have to do what I say now!"

"What?! No, that's not how this is going to work. You've never said anything like that before. You're joking, right? Please just let me sleep and we'll consummate our marriage in the morning."

He yelled, "No! It needs to be tonight!" Then he slapped me across the face.

I let out a shriek, in complete shock. He had never been violent before. "What did you just do?! Did you really just hit me?! We just got married and now you're trying to control me?" Crying, and shoving my face in the pillow, I said, "Please, please just let me sleep. I can't deal with this right now."

I cried myself to sleep on the edge of the bed and he passed out next to me, with his feet at the top of the bed, unwilling to even use body language to attempt to make amends.

The next morning, we checked out of our hotel and went to get coffee. As we were waiting to cross the street, he said, "I'm so sorry, babe. I love you so much. I was just really tired and stressed. I promise I'll never do anything like that again."

I squinted back at him, trying to read his face for clues. *Would he? I didn't think he would ever do that in the first place, so how do I know he won't do it again?*

I turned my head from side to side and looked around the city for a sign. *Madison. First. Starbucks. North Face.* The rain blurred the signs, but none that gave me any indication of what to do or what would happen in the future. I didn't know what to think or do, so I said, "Okay, honey. Let's just get some coffee and go enjoy our honeymoon."

"Babe, really, though? Do you believe me? I promise we'll have a happy life together, and I'll do everything I can to make you happy!" he said, seemingly earnestly while he pursed his lips for a kiss.

I bleakly smiled back and simply said, "Okay, thank you." I stared at the gray sky and drizzling rain. I couldn't see anything through it, and I gave up trying to see and understand.

I loved him, and this seemed unusual for him, so I accepted his apology and kissed him. This was just a freak accident, I told myself. I didn't want to end my marriage before it started, I told myself. I didn't want to give up on this life I created, I told myself. And then, I told myself maybe it was my fault I drank too much to have any energy left for him that night. I pushed the incident away to the smallest corner of my mind and didn't tell anyone. I was shocked and ashamed to have married someone that could hit me on our wedding night – or at all. I didn't even remember it happened until three years later when I walked by our wedding venue.

Chapter 11 Warning Signs

This chapter is about our wedding, yet it is full of warning signs and straight abuse. The first warning sign here is that even though I was stressed about the flowers and wanted his emotional support, I didn't want to bother him. In a healthy relationship, partners can call each other for emotional support and don't feel that they are bothering them to ask for it.

As an aside, the wedding logo that I mentioned designing is part of the cover image for this book. That logo is the front part of the image, and then later I made the image behind it to show how the relationship actually felt.

Back to the warning signs. I had previously been concerned about how much his family liked me, but when they gave me the engagement ring, I felt they were finally showing me that they did like me and support our relationship. Yet, when his sisters didn't make it to the nail appointment or to the hotel room to get ready together, I felt like they didn't care about me or our relationship enough to show up. In healthy relationships, when the families state that they support the relationship, they emotionally support the couple, are excited about showing their support, and show up to do so.

Just before we were about to get married, I started feeling incredibly anxious. Looking back, I think I was on the cusp of a panic attack. I was ignoring my instincts not to get married, and I was pushing myself to go through with it because it seemed like the logical decision to make at the time. My instincts were telling me there were warning signs, but I ignored them.

It *was* strange that I didn't immediately spot my fiancée in the crowd. I don't know if that is an explicit warning sign, but that was definitely not the case in other relationships I had been in.

It was certainly odd that he chose his wedding song as the *Imperial March*, the song from *Star Wars* about the villain. All of these little things that felt "odd" to me, could be seen as warning signs, but they were hard to pinpoint, which is likely why I ignored them. But, feeling that something is "odd" or "off" is an instinct, which should not be ignored.

He told me that I had to watch all of his favorite shows, which were interestingly all about mobsters and villains, in order to marry him. That could also be a warning sign, although many people enjoy those movies, and they are not abusers. I think it is important to look at these warning signs as accumulation of different problems. Looking at them individually, as I did at the time, made it easier for me to overlook them.

When Jason told me that I needed to watch all of those movies and TV shows, I saw it as the perfect time to ask him to help out more around the house. In a healthy relationship, both partners contribute to housework. However, studies show that on average, women contribute to more than 50 percent of the housework (cooking, cleaning, child rearing) than men do, which I knew at the time, so I also thought it was pretty "normal." What I didn't recognize was normal, was that I was doing over 90% of the cooking and cleaning. I knew I wanted his help, so I tried to get it through this "compromise," but even that didn't work. He manipulated me into doing everything. His lack of help with the wedding planning also shows more signs of him using his male privilege to get what he wants – which seemed to be to do nothing.

I was absolutely heartbroken that Jason did not take the time or emotional energy to write his own vows. It is tough when a warning sign like that shows up in the middle of a wedding ceremony. I felt as though I was already committed to him, and so even though I was devastated, I continued through with making my commitment to him and enjoying the rest of the wedding.

He told me that he got to have, "Pour Some Sugar on Me," as his song because it was a "strip club song" and he is the "man," which is another example of his adoration for the patriarchy and emotional abuse of "Using Male Privilege." I ended up choosing, "Addicted to Love." I think perhaps I was addicted to his love. By this time in our relationship, three years of being together, I was already under his spell and dependent upon him, which is likely a lot of the reason I overlooked his bad behavior. I also had not set any boundaries about what constituted acceptable or good behavior.

Even though I had previously made him promise that he would not shove cake in my face, he still pretended to do so. He didn't actually do it, but he said, "I told you I wouldn't do that, babe! Don't you trust me?" I recognized then, even if just for a split moment, that I didn't actually trust him. Yet, I laughed and tried to stay happy in the moment. The fact that I did not trust him was a huge warning sign.

It also seemed he did not trust me. He was often jealous when I talked to male friends or spent time with them. Yet, that night, he seemed to be okay with it, which made me feel perhaps he trusted me then because we were married. That made me feel better about the lack of trust, so I didn't think much of it after that. Although, lack of trust in a relationship is definitely a warning sign.

Jason hit me. That was not a warning sign of abuse, it was actual physical abuse. He hit me out of anger in an attempt to control me. He literally told me, "You are my wife! You have to do what I say now!" There is no disputing that he was trying to control me in that moment, and that he used physical force to attempt to do so.

It made it even more confusing that he hit me on our wedding night. Objectively, one can see this was wrong. I even knew it was wrong at the time. But I was already so much under his spell, that I began to self-blame for his actions. I victim-blamed myself, which is actually a very common reaction to abuse because the abusers manipulate the survivors into thinking the abuse is their fault. It is part of the way they gain control. If survivors think the violence is their fault, then they do not blame or leave the abusers. I think I partially fell for it because I was already dependent upon him for his love, and I am empathic, so I looked at the situation from his eyes. In his eyes, I was in the wrong for not wanting to consummate our marriage on our wedding night. At the time, I saw the world through his eyes and my own rose-colored glasses.

Volume 1 Epilogue

Take a breath. Congratulate yourself for making it through this far. Take a look at the resources and suggested books in the last few pages. Process your thoughts and what you learned. Share your thoughts and experiences with the community on #WarningSigns. When you are ready, read Volume 2 and learn more about how abuse occurs and why people stay in abusive relationships.

Volume 1 Warning Signs

This is a list of the warning signs from this volume. The warning signs about his behaviors are in normal font, and the warning signs about my feelings and actions are in italic font. Actual abuse is in bold font. Some behaviors are difficult to differentiate between being a warning sign, emotional abuse, or physical abuse. Physical abuse also includes threats. My interpretations of the behaviors are just that; some people may have different interpretations of which items fit into which categories and that is okay. It is also possible that I missed some of the signs, and even abuse. Write in #WarningSigns and let me know.

Chapter 1
- No warning signs yet

Chapter 2
- Codependency
- Love bombing
- Possibly selfish because he only talked about what he wanted to discuss
- Awkward family dynamics as a possible warning sign

Chapter 3

- Selfish, didn't care about me being hungry
- Codependency, quickly falling in love
- Selfish, didn't consider I wanted to spend time with my family too
- Silenced my voice and opinions
- *I ignored my intuition*
- His family discussed missing his ex in front of me
- His family didn't accept me
- *I stuffed my feelings*

Chapter 4

- Codependency, moved in together after just 3 months
- At the beginning, he agreed with whatever I wanted
- A few months later, he never considered what I wanted
- He only played violent video games where he killed realistic-looking people
- *I felt so confused I was nauseous, and ignored that gut feeling*
- He ignored that I was feeling ill
- He manipulated me into making all the moving plans and doing all the packing
- *It felt easier to go along with whatever he wanted; I was slowly losing myself to him*

Chapter 5

- Selfish, didn't help with moving and packing
- Strong sense of patriarchy, he felt insecure about me paying for everything, seeing the kitchen as women's territory and fixing the car as men's
- **Isolation: Saying it would be nice to just be by ourselves, didn't let me call my friends and family**
- Unhealthy family dynamic, his parents putting him in the middle of their arguing
- *My anxiety due to ignoring my instincts*
- *I didn't feel comfortable about the way I was being treated*
- **Minimizing: He minimized all I was doing and how I felt about it being uneven**
- He manipulated his friend to do all the driving
- **Intimidation: He used violence on inanimate objects, his laptop and car tire**

Chapter 6

- He didn't show empathy for the customer's experience or my experience trying to help her
- He made sexist and racist remarks
- **Emotional abuse: putting me down, making me feel bad**

- He was not supportive
- **Emotional abuse: He made me feel guilty for taking time to find a better job**
- **Emotional abuse: Brought down my self confidence, created dependency on him for a source of happiness**

Chapter 7

- **Emotional abuse: Name calling**
- **Emotional abuse: Putting me down**
- Easily angered
- *I ignored what bothered me, and put energy into what was going well*
- *I felt responsible for his happiness*
- **Emotional abuse: Taking control of conversations, creating the power dynamic**
- Sexism
- **Emotional abuse: Lack of respect for partner**
- **Emotional abuse: Bring them down, bring them back up again, creating dependency, emotional cycle of violence**

Chapter 8

- **Emotional abuse: "Jokes" and "teasing" make you feel bad**

- *Being so determined to continue forward without listening to instincts*
- *Having to prove myself to him*
- *Felt guilty for overwhelming him, but actually just stating my desires for the future*

Chapter 9

- Feigning confusion to placate him
- **Emotional abuse: name calling, calling my fingers fat**
- *Ignoring the emotional abuse*
- He "let us" go to my favorite place to celebrate
- *Compromising with him, toward the point of dependency*

Chapter 10

- Only allowed me to talk about things at certain times
- *Did not set boundaries for myself*
  - I didn't set boundaries, but if I had and they weren't respected this would also be a warning sign
- Manipulated me to do all the work
- Feeling the relationship is one-sided

Chapter 11

- *Feeling you can't go to your partner for emotional support*
- *Feeling anxious, cusp of panic attack, perhaps panic attack, ignoring warning signs*
- His family didn't show emotional support
- *Feeling something is odd or off and ignoring those feelings*
- He plagiarized his vows and did not put in emotional energy to writing them
- *Feeling of not trusting your partner*
- **Physical abuse: He actually hit me**

Epilogue

The <u>Women Against Abuse website</u> (2022) states that it takes people an average of seven times to leave their abusers. Other sources cite this number as high as thirty times. I am so grateful that I was able to do it in just one time. But I could likely point out far more than thirty counts of abuse before I actually left. I include this information so that people recognize how common it is to take a long time for survivors to actually leave their abusers for good.

If you think someone you know is being abused, tell them. It might feel scary, and it might feel that you are risking losing that relationship with that person. They might not do anything about it right away. They will likely eventually do something on their own time, although not everyone is so lucky; some people who are abused end up killed by their abusers. Most people will eventually leave, though, and the sooner you tell them about the abuse you notice the sooner they will leave and be safe. The bottom line is that the person's life is more important than your relationship with them. It is an issue of safety over trust. Helping the survivor become safe is more important than this person temporarily feeling they cannot trust you. Eventually, they will see that you helped them save themselves and they will be grateful.

It is vital that survivors make the decision to leave in ways that feel safe for them. As mentioned before, there is a high risk of murder when a survivor leaves a a partner. Therefore, it is literally vital that survivors make the decision to leave when it is safe, and in the safest possible way for them. Domestic violence and intimate partner violence advocates can help people make individualized safety plans, which are detailed plans for safely leaving their abusers.

It is also crucial for people supporting survivors to understand that their abusers broke down their confidence in such a way that it not only prevented them from leaving, but that it broke down their sense of autonomy; that is, their ability to make decisions for themselves. So, when people help survivors make the decisions necessary to leave, they must ensure that the survivor ultimately makes decisions on their own.

This does three things: One, it decreases the chance of the survivor returning to their abuser. Two, it helps the survivor make decisions in safe ways that preserve their lives. Three, it helps the survivor learn to heal and find themselves again.

There are also two things that support people can tell survivors to help them make decisions to leave. One, is that abusers do not change. Very few abusers get help to change, which is usually in the form of a court-mandated support group. Those that do attend those groups, tend to learn tactics about how to become more effective abusers instead of actually changing. Two, abusers do not actually love their survivors. People that intentionally hurt people do not abuse them. Period. This is very difficult for survivors to hear, because they were so engrossed in that message of love, the cycle of violence, and their trauma bond that it kept them intertwined with them. The sooner that survivors can recognize that abusers do not actually love them, the sooner they can take the steps to leave them.

Bill of Rights

This is the survivor's Bill of Rights. New Beginnings survivors read this aloud together after every support group (other support groups also use it). I keep a copy of it on my refrigerator so I can always be reminded. One can also view these rights as "green flags" in their relationships. If they are being respected, then that is a sign of a healthy relationship. If they are not respected, then that is a warning sign. I recommend that all humans read it and allow it to become part of their daily lives. Everyone deserves to live their lives with these basic human rights.

My Bill Of Rights

I have the right to be me.

I have the right to put myself first.

I have the right to be safe.

I have the right to love and be loved.

I have the right to be treated with respect.

I have the right to be human, not perfect.

I have the right to be angry and protest if I am treated unfairly or abusively by anyone I have the right to my own privacy.

I have the right to my own opinions, to express them and to be taken seriously.

I have the right to earn and control my own money.

I have the right to ask questions about anything that affects my life.

I have the right to make decisions that affect me.

I have the right to grow and change (and that includes my mind).

I have the right to say "No".

I have the right to make mistakes.

I have the right NOT to be responsible for other adult's problems.

I have the right not to be liked by everyone.

I have the right to control my own life and to change it if I am not happy with it as it is .

Thank you for reading this. Please follow me on social media @katemageau.counselor and visit my website at www.katemageau.com to learn more about DV and IPV, find links and information about my other books, and learn about my individual and group counseling, coaching and consulting, and workshops.

Resources

Centers for Disease Control information on domestic violence:
https://www.cdc.gov/violenceprevention/intimatepartnerviolence/fastfact.html

Cycle of violence: https://domesticviolence.org/cycle-of-violence/

Love Bombing:
https://www.healthline.com/health/love-bombing

National Domestic Violence Hotline:
1-800-799-SAFE (7233) https://www.thehotline.org/

Power and control wheel:
http://www.ncdsv.org/images/powercontrolwheelnoshading.pdf

Psychology Today Therapist Finder:
https://www.psychologytoday.com/us/therapists

Recommended Books

Codependency No More by Melodie Beattie
The Betrayal Bond by Patrick Carnes, PhD.
The Body Keeps the Score by Bessel van der Kolk, M.D.
Trauma and Recovery by Judith Herman
What Happened to You? by Oprah Winfrey and Bruce D. Perry, M.D., PhD.
Why Does He Do That? Inside the Minds of Angry and Controlling Men by Lundy Bancroft

References

American Psychiatric Association. (2013). *Diagnostic and statistical manual of mental disorders (5th ed.).* Washington, DC: Author.

Domestic Abuse Intervention Project (n.d). *Power and control wheel.* National Center on Domestic and Sexual Violence. http://www.ncdsv.org/images/powercontrolwheelnoshading.pdf

Fast facts: Preventing intimate partner violence. (2022). Centers for Disease Control and Prevention. https://www.cdc.gov/violenceprevention/intimatepartnerviolence/fastfact.html

Lamonthe, C. (2022). *Love bombing: 10 signs of over the top love.* Healthline. https://www.healthline.com/health/love-bombing

Miller, E., & Brigid, M. (2019). Intimate partner violence. *The New England Journal of Medicine, 380*(9), 850-857. http://dx.doi.org/10.1056/NEJMra1807166

National Domestic Violence Hotline. https://www.thehotline.org/

O'Doherty, L. J., Taft, A., Hegarty, K., Ramsay, J., Davidson, L. L., & Feder, G. (2014). Screening women for intimate partner violence in healthcare settings: abridged Cochrane systematic review and meta-analysis. *BMJ: British Medical Journal, 348.* https://www.jstor.org/stable/26514759

Perry, D.B. & Winfrey, O. (2021). *What Happened to You?* Flat Iron Publishing.

Step by step guide to understanding the cycle of violence. (2022). Domestic Violence: It's Everybody's Business. https://domesticviolence.org/cycle-of-violence/

What is domestic abuse? (2022) *United* Nations Covid-19 Response. https://www.un.org/en/coronavirus/what-is-domestic-abuse

Why it's so difficult to leave. (2022). Women Against Abuse. https://www.womenagainstabuse.org/education-resources/learn-about-abuse/why-its-so-difficult-to-leave

Made in the USA
Columbia, SC
12 October 2024